whale done

Also by Stuart Gibbs

The Spy School series

Spy School

Spy Camp

Evil Spy School

Spy Ski School

Spy School Secret Service

Spy School Goes South

Spy School British Invasion

Spy School Revolution

Spy School at Sea

Spy School Project X

With Anjan Sarkar
*Spy School
the Graphic Novel*

*Spy Camp
the Graphic Novel*

The FunJungle series

Belly Up

Poached

Big Game

Panda-monium

Lion Down

Tyrannosaurus Wrecks

Bear Bottom

The Moon Base Alpha series

Space Case

Spaced Out

Waste of Space

The Charlie Thorne series

*Charlie Thorne and the
Last Equation*

*Charlie Thorne and the
Lost City*

*Charlie Thorne and the
Curse of Cleopatra*

The Once Upon a Tim series

Once Upon a Tim

The Labyrinth of Doom

The Last Musketeer

STUART GIBBS

whale done

A **funjungle** NOVEL

Simon & Schuster Books for Young Readers

New York London Toronto Sydney New Delhi

SIMON & SCHUSTER BOOKS FOR YOUNG READERS
An imprint of Simon & Schuster Children's Publishing Division
1230 Avenue of the Americas, New York, New York 10020

For information about special discounts for bulk purchases, please contact Simon & Schuster Special Sales at 1-866-506-1949 or business@simonandschuster.com.
The Simon & Schuster Speakers Bureau can bring authors to your live event. For more information or to book an event, contact the Simon & Schuster Speakers Bureau at 1-866-248-3049 or visit our website at www.simonspeakers.com.
Interior design by Lucy Ruth Cummins
Endpaper art by Ryan Thompson
The text for this book was set in Adobe Garamond Pro.
Manufactured in the United States of America
0123 FFG
First Edition
10 9 8 7 6 5 4 3 2 1
Library of Congress Cataloging-in-Publication Data
Names: Gibbs, Stuart, 1969– author.
Title: Whale done : a FunJungle novel / Stuart Gibbs.
Description: First edition. | New York : Simon & Schuster Books for Young Readers, [2023] | Audience: Ages 8–12. | Audience: Grades 4–6. |
Summary: While visiting his girlfriend Summer in Malibu, Teddy stumbles upon two mysteries involving a blown up whale explosion and a string of beach sand thefts, but his investigation is sidetracked by a rumor that his girlfriend is dating a celebrity, leading him to question their relationship.
Identifiers: LCCN 2022023911 (print) | LCCN 2022023912 (ebook) |
ISBN 9781534499317 (hardcover) | ISBN 9781534499331 (ebook)
Subjects: CYAC: Mystery and detective stories. | Stealing—Fiction. |
Beaches—Fiction. | Dating—Fiction. | LCGFT: Detective and mystery fiction. | Novels.
Classification: LCC PZ7.G339236 Wh 2023 (print) | LCC PZ7.G339236 (ebook) |
DDC [Foc]—dc23
LC record available at https://lccn.loc.gov/2022023911
LC ebook record available at https://lccn.loc.gov/2022023912

For Marc Zachary, who knows more about theme parks (and plenty of other stuff) than just about anyone. Thanks for all the advice over the years.

Contents

whale done

THE ESCAPE

I would never have seen the whale explode if a kangaroo hadn't burned down my house.

The kangaroo was a four-year-old male named Hopalong Cassidy, and the fire wasn't entirely his fault. It's not like kangaroos go around plotting arson. All that Hopalong was truly guilty of was trying to escape.

I know this because I witnessed the entire event.

My name is Teddy Fitzroy. I'm fourteen years old, and I live at FunJungle Wild Animal Park.

FunJungle is the most popular tourist attraction in all of Texas, an enormous theme park and zoo featuring many of the finest animal exhibits ever built. Both my parents work there—my mother is the head primatologist, while my father is the official photographer—and because their jobs require them to be at FunJungle at all hours, we have employee housing.

But while FunJungle had spared no expense to create incredible habitats for the animals, with state-of-the-art facilities and innovative designs, the park had really skimped when it came to providing lodging for humans. The public relations department had named the staff housing area Lakeside Estates, but it was merely a group of mobile homes haphazardly arranged in the woods behind the employee parking lot. They were supposed to be deluxe models, but my father suspected they were actually defective merchandise that the dealer hadn't been able to sell. (J.J. McCracken, the billionaire owner of FunJungle, also owned the mobile home company.) Our home was slightly lopsided, with bargain-basement appliances and walls so thin you could hear what neighbors were watching on television. Even worse, the utilities were barely functional. The septic system often smelled worse than the elephant house, and the electricity conked out on a regular basis.

Which was why I wasn't home during the fire. The mobile home park had suffered a power failure—on the hottest day of the year, no less.

Central Texas is known for being hot and humid, but that mid-August day was brutal. The state was suffering through its worst heat wave in a decade, and that afternoon it had been

116 degrees in the shade. Even animals that lived in deserts, like the camels and fennec foxes, seemed to think this was too much and refused to go outside. Despite this, the park was still busy; it was the height of tourist season, and parents who had built up the trip for weeks didn't have the heart to tell their children they weren't going. (In addition, many guests had prepaid for nonrefundable park admission packages.) But everyone who had dared to venture outdoors looked miserable. They slouched about in the heat, gulping down overpriced sodas to stay hydrated and griping that none of the animals were doing anything but napping. The Polar Pavilion, which was refrigerated to arctic temperatures for the polar bears and penguins, had a two-hour line to get inside.

I had spent most of the day with my best friend, Xavier, and my girlfriend, Summer, trying to find ways to stay cool. Xavier was a junior volunteer at FunJungle, and though his shift at the giraffe feeding station had been canceled due to the heat, he still came to work because he was a wannabe field biologist, and FunJungle was his favorite place on earth. Meanwhile, Summer was the daughter of J.J. McCracken. All three of us had befriended many FunJungle employees over the past year, so we were able to finagle our way into the VIP lane for the Raging Rapids ride, which we went on so many times in a row that I lost count.

After repeated drenching, our clothes were so waterlogged,

we thought we might be able to stay cool enough to ride out the rest of the afternoon in my trailer, even with its anemic air-conditioning. Lakeside Estates was located only a short walk from the theme park rides at FunJungle. But as we approached my house, the power blew.

We could tell by the sound. Everyone who was home had their air conditioners going full blast. One second, the machines were all humming so loud, it sounded like we were inside an enormous wasps' nest—and then, suddenly, everything went silent. Two seconds after *that*, the profanity began. We could hear everyone through their paper-thin walls as they cursed the lousy power system, the cheap air conditioners, and Summer's father, who had skimped on building the place.

We happened to be directly outside the trailer of Drew Filus, the chief ornithologist, when he unleashed an extremely long stream of insults about J.J. McCracken, and then made a few shocking suggestions about what J.J. could do with the crummy air conditioners he had bought. It went on for a good three minutes.

"Sorry you had to hear that," I said to Summer, once it had finally ended.

She shrugged, unconcerned. "I've heard far worse than that about Dad."

Even though it was getting late in the afternoon, it was

still miserably hot. My clothes had already dried out, save for my soggy shoes and damp underwear. Evidence of the drought was all around us: the ground was parched, the grass was brown and brittle, and the tiny pond that FunJungle public relations amusingly referred to as a lake had completely evaporated, leaving only a stretch of dried-out mud.

"Guess the trailer is out of commission," Xavier observed morosely. "Where to now?"

"Maybe my dad's office?" Summer suggested. "I'm sure the administration building still has air-conditioning. The whole park has backup generators."

"Except employee housing," I groused. The administration building was all the way on the other side of FunJungle, a twenty-minute walk through the heat. Standing around and griping wasn't going to make things any better, though, so we started back through the desiccated woods toward FunJungle's rear employee entrance.

Our route took us through the staff parking lot, a wide stretch of simmering asphalt that felt like the Sahara as we crossed it. Numerous employees were headed home for the day, but their cars were so hot after baking in the sun for hours that no one could get right in and drive away. Instead, most had started their vehicles and were letting them run with the windows open and the air-conditioning cranked, waiting for them to cool down.

Kevin Wilkes was standing in the shade of his rusted pickup truck, killing time by setting off leftover fireworks from the Fourth of July.

Kevin was one of the dimmer FunJungle employees. He had originally been hired as a security guard but had lost that job after I discovered he'd been unwittingly feeding the giraffes local plants that were making them sick. Now Kevin had been demoted to janitorial work in the FunJungle Emporium, as it was about as far away from the animals as you could get.

In the month before Independence Day, fireworks stands sprouted like weeds along highways all through Texas. Kevin had blown an entire week's pay on several crates, planning to put on an epic fireworks display to impress a woman he liked at his apartment complex, but the complex had banned him from doing it, rightfully fearing disaster. They also refused to let him store the fireworks in his apartment, as it was a violation of three dozen safety codes. So Kevin had been stuck with several thousand low-quality fireworks, which he kept in the bed of his pickup.

When we came across him, he had just lit a few spinners, which were whirling and sparking on the asphalt. "Hey!" he called out to us. "Want to set off some fireworks?"

"You shouldn't be doing that," Summer told him. "The woods around here could catch fire in an instant."

Normally, zoos try to time the delivery of animals after official hours, so there aren't tourists around, but FunJungle stayed open much later than normal zoos, and, while the truck that was delivering Hopalong was air-conditioned, the veterinary staff still didn't want to keep an animal locked inside a vehicle on a hot day any longer than they had to.

In recent years, zoos across the United States had recognized that kangaroos—and their close relatives, wallabies—were so docile that they could be displayed in a way that most other animals could not: in large enclosures that visitors could actually walk through. FunJungle had quickly jumped on the bandwagon and was modifying its Australian area to feature an exhibit like this. The Land Down Under would allow guests to wander a path right through the marsupial habitat. It was scheduled to open in the fall, and in the meantime, FunJungle was trying to acquire every kangaroo and wallaby it could.

Hopalong was a western gray kangaroo who had been born at the Milwaukee Zoo. At four years old, he was already mature, six and a half feet tall and 120 pounds. He had a reputation for being good-tempered and comfortable around humans, although the FunJungle staff was still taking every precaution to ensure that nothing went wrong. Hopalong had been delivered in a specially designed trailer with plenty of room for him to move about during his long drive from Milwaukee, but the truck was too big to drive through the park to the Land Down Under. So Hopalong was being transferred into a crate on a smaller truck in the employee parking lot, which would then take him through the behind-the-scenes area to his new home. Luring Hopalong from his comfortable, air-conditioned trailer into the crate out in the heat was a delicate process. In their natural habitat in Australia, wild kangaroos could occasionally face temperatures as hot as it was that day, but Hopalong was used to the milder weather of Wisconsin. The keepers were trying to coax him with biscuits that had been developed in the FunJungle kitchens to appeal to kangaroos.

Hopalong had just been edging from the trailer into the crate when the poppers went off.

Not only was the kangaroo startled, but his handlers were too. They quickly took cover, leaving the crate unsecured in the back of the truck. It shifted slightly, so that it was no longer flush with the trailer. Instead, there was a gap of a few inches.

Hopalong immediately took advantage of this.

A kangaroo's huge hind legs are incredibly strong. The animals can cover twenty-five feet in a single leap, jump six feet vertically, or travel at thirty-five miles per hour for short bursts. Hopalong wedged one of his enormous feet into the gap and, with a quick flex of his leg muscles, sent the crate skidding back into the truck.

Then he dropped to the ground and bounded across the parking lot, fleeing for the woods.

His route took him directly toward me and my friends.

Summer, Xavier, and I scrambled out of his way. You never want to stand in the path of a big animal. An herbivore can really hurt you if it runs into you at full speed.

Kevin, on the other hand, didn't even see Hopalong coming.

He was busily lighting some sparklers and backed directly into Hopalong's way. The kangaroo pivoted to avoid a head-on collision, but his powerful tail thwacked Kevin in the chest.

A kangaroo's tail is almost as powerful as its legs. Hopalong's was a thick club of taut muscle, and it sent Kevin reeling backward. The sparklers flew from Kevin's hand and landed in the bed of his truck. . . .

Right in a crate of unused fireworks.

"Uh-oh," Kevin said.

"Get away!" I yelled, then grabbed Summer's hand and raced across the parking lot.

Xavier and Kevin were right on our heels.

Behind us, the crate of fireworks erupted. Hundreds of roman candles, fountains, and aerial repeaters went off at once. Spinners crackled and poppers burst while rockets and colored balls of light blasted into the sky. So many fireworks were detonating that the truck trembled as though it were at ground zero in an earthquake.

All the noise spooked Hopalong even more. The kangaroo bolted out of the parking lot and down the road that led to the park exit.

Kevin had sprung for a few expensive fireworks—the type that professionals would use in their shows—and those now exploded in the air high above, creating floral blooms and starbursts. The sizzling embers rained down around us. A few landed in the drought-parched woods that surrounded employee housing.

Which was how the forest fire began.

THE INFERNO

The forest around FunJungle was a tinderbox.

The ground was covered with a thick carpet of dead leaves and dry grass. All it needed to ignite was a spark—and thanks to the impromptu fireworks display, there were plenty of those. Dozens of small fires sprouted within seconds, and those quickly merged into larger and larger blazes.

It was immediately evident that this was going to be a problem.

Most of the FunJungle employees who had been waiting for their cars to cool off decided it was time to go. They leaped into their vehicles and raced out of the parking lot. In their haste, several banged into one another, scraping the sides of their cars and shearing off rearview mirrors, but no one bothered to stop. Kevin was among them. He foolishly sped off in his truck, apparently forgetting that fireworks were still going off in the bed. They continued to spew out and explode, setting off more fires along the exit road.

The original fire was growing quickly on the edge of the parking lot, threatening to cut off access to the employee housing. Thick smoke billowed into the air, and the crackle of flame was so loud, we had to shout over it.

"We need to warn everyone in Lakeside Estates about the fire!" Xavier yelled. He started toward the woods, but Summer grabbed his arm, holding him there.

"It's burning too fast!" she warned. "If we go that way, we'll get trapped!"

Both of them turned to me, waiting for my opinion.

I considered the growing blaze carefully, then shook my head. "Summer's right. It's too risky." I felt terrible about saying it, but I also knew that we had no training for how to survive in a fire like this.

"But there's people in danger!" Xavier protested. "They need to be warned!"

I pointed to the thick column of smoke rising into the air. "I think they already know."

A second later, the emergency alert system at FunJungle activated. Throughout the park, there were thousands of speakers. Most of the time, they played recorded noises like frog croaks and bird calls to enhance the feeling of being in nature—or local cultural music to match the nearby exhibits, like Maasai tribal chants in the African plains or wailing didgeridoos in Australia. Now they blasted a series of short, loud alarms to get the attention of all guests, followed by an urgent announcement:

"This is an emergency alert. It is currently necessary to evacuate FunJungle Wild Animal Park. Please proceed calmly and slowly to the closest emergency exit. You are in no immediate danger, so please do not panic."

The announcement had been recorded by a woman who had an exceptionally soothing voice so that guests would not freak out when they heard it.

It didn't work.

The moment the announcement ended, shrieks of terror rang out from all over the park. Many guests could already see the smoke from the fire, and now that the emergency announcement had sounded, they went into the exact sort of panic that we were hoping to avoid. Crowds stampeded toward the front gates, even though there were plenty of other emergency exits. People pushed one another aside, trampled shortcuts through the landscaping, and shoved over any obstacles in their path: trash cans, food kiosks, and the unfortunate employees dressed as mascots.

FunJungle had a dozen different animal characters, each with its own costume, which actors would wear to amuse young children. It was one of the worst jobs at the park, as the costumes were bulky, heavy, and hot on a normal day; on a scorcher like this, they were practically torture devices. It was difficult to even walk in the top-heavy outfits, let alone run, and now the poor actors found themselves swarmed by fleeing guests. Zelda Zebra was upended into a copse of lavender bushes, Eleanor Elephant was smashed into a wall so hard that her trunk came off, and Larry the Lizard was knocked into the duck pond, where he was immediately besieged by angry mallards. While fleeing a crush of stampeding tourists, Kazoo the Koala literally lost her head: the bulbous object tore off the costume and rolled down a hill, traumatizing several kindergarteners who mistakenly believed that their favorite FunJungle character had been decapitated.

But while the tourists' behavior was deplorable, the Fun-Jungle Fire Department acted heroically.

J.J. McCracken had been concerned about fire from day one, given that his park was located on the edge of several square miles of drought-prone wilderness. So FunJungle had its own fire department (as well as its own security force and medical team). There was also an elaborate system of water lines and hydrants, and each animal habitat had twice the regulated number of fire sprinklers. (These could also be used to keep the animals cool on hot days, and so had been in repeated use over the past week.) In addition to the five full-time firefighters, much of the Fun-Jungle staff had extensive training for fire safety, and two dozen employees were deputized as volunteer firefighters—including my father. Due to these precautions, there hadn't been a major blaze at FunJungle since the park had opened. (Although careless guests had started a few small ones, usually by tossing lit cigarettes into the garbage.) Except for drills, both of FunJungle's fire trucks had never been used—until that day.

The fire station was located in the rear of FunJungle in order to be close to the forest, and thus, the biggest threat of fire. So it wasn't long before the engines pulled into the employee parking lot, sirens wailing. The firefighters went right to work hooking hoses to the hydrants. But even in that short span, the blaze had grown surprisingly fast. The trees along the edge of the lot were blazing, and thick curtains of smoke rolled across the asphalt.

Xavier, Summer, and I hurried through them to talk to Chief Benson, who was a tough, no-nonsense woman in her fifties. She shouted at us as we approached. "You kids shouldn't be anywhere around here! The best thing you can do to help is to leave this to us!"

"There's still people in employee housing!" Xavier shouted back. "Over there!" He pointed through the flames.

Chief Benson immediately grew concerned. "Any idea how many?"

Xavier, Summer, and I looked to one another, unsure. "We don't know," I admitted. "Drew Filus was definitely in his house. And we heard a few others."

"Maybe five or six?" Summer suggested.

"We'll get them out." Chief Benson spoke so confidently that I believed her. "Now leave this to us!"

We nodded in agreement and hurried back across the parking lot while the chief bravely led a team into the inferno.

Between the heat of the day and the heat of the fire, I was as hot as I had ever been in my life. My skin felt as though my entire body had just touched an iron. I was amazed that the firefighters could even function in their heavy fireproof clothing.

My phone buzzed in my pocket. I wasn't surprised to find that it was my mother. I answered. "Don't worry. I'm safe."

"Please tell me that you're nowhere near that fire."

I didn't even consider lying to her; Mom could always tell. "Actually, I was right nearby when it started. . . ."

Mom sighed heavily. "Of course you were. Any time there's trouble, you're right in the middle of it."

There was no point in denying this. Ever since we had moved to FunJungle, I had attracted trouble like a magnet.

At first, this had been my fault, as I had taken it upon myself to investigate the murder of FunJungle's mascot, Henry the Hippo, not realizing how much danger I would end up in. However, I had solved that mystery, which led to my involvement in several others—and lots more danger. Even when I did my best to be cautious, I still ended up in plenty of peril.

"I'm not in the middle this time," I assured my mother. "I'm just on the sidelines."

"It certainly *sounds* like you're in the middle of it. And I'd like you as far away as possible. Come to my office. It's safe here."

Mom's office was in Monkey Mountain, a building filled with primate habitats in the center of the park. It certainly would have been a good place to escape the fire—and as a bonus, it was very well air-conditioned—but to get there meant heading back into the park again. Passing through the employee entrance would have been almost impossible, as hundreds of people were streaming out through it, after which we would have to face the hordes of panicked guests rampaging through the park.

"I'm not sure I can get to you," I told my mother. "I think the tourists might be more dangerous than the fire."

"That's a good point." Mom spoke with the resigned tone of a woman who regularly chastised park guests for tormenting the monkeys. "How crazy is it out there?"

Over the fence, I watched the tourists streaming past. Some were screaming. Some were crying. Many were shoving their fellow humans out of the way. One frantic father was swatting everyone else with a Henry Hippo plush doll. I overheard the radio of a nearby security officer, where a report came in that dozens of tourists fearing the fire had leaped into the dolphin pool, unaware that Snickers, one of the male dolphins, liked to steal people's shorts. So now, in addition to being frightened by the fire, they were also freaking out because they'd been pantsed.

"On a scale of one to ten," I said, "it's a hundred and twenty."

Mom groaned. "All right. Stay away from the crowds. *And* the fire. Your father's probably going to be there soon."

Sure enough, Dad was exiting the park at that moment, on his way to join the other volunteer firefighters. I waved to him while telling Mom, "I see him."

"Make sure he doesn't do anything stupid either," Mom said, only half joking. Then she added, "I love you."

"Love you too." I hung up as Dad came over.

"I should have known you'd be in the thick of this," he said.

"Mom already gave me an earful," I told him. "And I've kept my distance."

"Doesn't look like it." Dad ran a finger down my face, then

held it up to show me that the tip was now coated with soot.

I hadn't realized how dirty I was. I looked to Summer and Xavier and realized they were both coated in soot as well.

"Teddy's telling the truth," Xavier insisted.

"Right," Dad said, obviously not believing him. "Stay over here. If this thing gets any worse, we might need your help to start evacuating animals." He raced over to the fire engines, where the firefighters had already hooked the hoses up and opened the hydrants.

Torrents of water gushed into the flames, which were burning so hot that the water seemed to instantly turn to steam. Still, the firefighters managed to clear a path through the blaze and then keep the inferno at bay on both sides.

Six people emerged through the smoke with Chief Benson at the lead: the other residents from employee housing. They were black with soot and coughing from the smoke but otherwise seemed okay.

A cheer went up from the gathered crowd.

But the battle wasn't over yet. Not by a long shot.

It would take until nearly six o'clock the next morning before the firefighters fully doused the blaze. To do it, they needed the help of four local fire stations, a squad of smoke jumpers, and three forest service helicopters, which scooped up water from the fake lake around the Raging Rapids ride and dropped it onto the flames.

Their heroic efforts protected the entirety of FunJungle. Not a single animal had to be evacuated—although hundreds of tourists had been hurt in the panicked flight to the exits. (None badly, thankfully; it was mostly bruises, scrapes, and one broken arm.) There was some damage to FunJungle's landscaping, mascot costumes, and a few kiosks, but overall, the park came out well.

However, the forest nearby was an entirely different story. The underbrush had been incinerated, and the trees had been torched. Hours before, the woods had been so thick with growth that much of it was nearly impenetrable; now there was nothing but barren ground and gnarled, blackened tree trunks. Ash rained down for miles around, but the thickest accumulations were in the burned forest, where great swaths of ground were carpeted in white, making it look bizarrely as if it were a snowy winter day, rather than a sultry summer one.

The blaze had been so hot when it tore through Lakeside Estates that almost nothing remained of our homes. The aluminum sides of the trailers had melted, and almost everything inside had vaporized, so all that was left were the warped metal hulks of our appliances and the concrete foundations.

Luckily, my family hadn't lost much—because we didn't own much to begin with. The first ten years of my life had been spent in a tent camp in the Congo while Mom studied primates, and we hadn't accumulated many possessions since moving to America. All our furniture, cookware, and appliances had been provided by FunJungle. My parents had kept their computers and Dad's photographic equipment in their offices, fearing exactly this sort of disaster—as well as thieves. (FunJungle had far better security than Lakeside Estates did.) So our losses were mostly limited to clothes, games, and books. But even so, as I stood among the wreckage the next day, I felt violated.

I had never been a big fan of the trailer, but still, it was home.

And now it was gone.

THE BEACH

There were two weeks until school started, and I didn't have a place to live.

Mom had work, and Dad was leaving for Argentina in two days to photograph guanacos for *National Geographic*. The resort hotels at FunJungle were booked solid, and the next nearest places to stay were some cheap motels along the highway twenty miles away. Mom figured that, in a pinch, she could put an air mattress in her office, but it wasn't big enough for two people. Xavier said I could stay with him, but he lived in a mobile home as well, with his parents and two younger sisters, so I knew that it was a big imposition for me to stay there. My next closest friends, Dashiell and Ethan, were away at football training camp for another week. And while the McCrackens had plenty of room at their home,

Summer was about to go on vacation to Malibu with her mother, and I wasn't comfortable staying alone with J.J.

Summer was the one who proposed the solution.

"Teddy should come with Mom and me to California," she told my parents.

We were at the site of what had been our home the next evening, sifting through the remnants to see if we could find anything of value. Around us, the other residents of employee housing were doing the same. Although the fire was out, the surrounding forest still smelled like it was burning. The scent was overpowering.

My parents turned to Summer, unsure. "We can't ask that of you . . . ," Mom began.

"It's no big deal," Summer said quickly. "We're staying at a friend's house, and it has like seventeen bedrooms. Teddy could have his own wing."

"And then there's plane fare . . . ," Dad said.

"Not an issue. We're taking the jet."

Mom and Dad shared a look. I could tell they were uncomfortable with accepting another free vacation from the McCrackens; their family had already taken all of us to Yellowstone that summer, not to mention having me over for dinner dozens of times and treating me to movies, concerts, and multiple trips to Schlitterbahn Waterpark in New Braunfels. I had felt a little weird about having Summer pay for everything at first, but she had ultimately told me that her family had more money than they knew what to do with, whereas mine did not, so I should stop fretting and enjoy it.

Despite their wealth, the McCrackens did not live ostentatiously. Instead of a mansion, they had a ranch house (albeit a very large ranch house on an extremely large ranch). Instead of limos and sports cars, they traveled in pickup trucks and hybrid SUVs. Summer bought the same clothes her friends did, from shops at the mall and thrift stores. But the McCrackens *did* splurge when it came to air travel. The jet was officially owned by one of J.J.'s many companies, but the family used it plenty. It was easy to understand why; my parents and I had taken the jet to Yellowstone with them, and it had been very nice.

Summer sensed my parents' hesitance and nudged them. "Bringing Teddy won't cost us anything extra. We're paying for the jet anyhow, so it doesn't matter if there are three people flying or four."

"Four people?" Dad echoed. "I thought your father wasn't going on this trip."

"He's not. But Doc is coming with us."

Mom looked up from a pile of ash she was sifting through, surprised. "Doc is going on vacation with you?"

Doc Deakin was the head vet at FunJungle. While he was renowned for the care and concern he showed animals, he was the opposite where humans were concerned. Except for his daughter and my mother, he generally seemed to be annoyed by the presence of every other human on earth.

"It's not a vacation for Doc," Summer explained. "A marine mammal center in Long Beach rescued a sea lion that some awful fisherman shot in the face. It's blind now, and they can't rehabilitate it, so Doc's going out to see about bringing it to FunJungle."

My parents and I cringed; even though we had heard thousands of stories of humans doing terrible things to animals, they never stopped being upsetting. Mom also seemed bothered by another part of the story. "That sounds like the sort of thing Doc would normally send an intern to do. Assuming he'd deign to send someone from the veterinary staff at all. It seems more like a transport issue than a medical one. So why is Doc going?"

Summer shrugged. "Maybe he thinks he can save the sea lion's eyesight or something?"

"I suppose," Mom said, although she didn't seem convinced.

A sob cut through the stillness of the day. Bonnie Melton, the head elephant keeper, was standing in the space where her trailer had been, clutching the remains of a charred photo album. It was amazing that any of it had survived the blaze at all—and yet, obviously, the damage was devastating.

Bonnie's wife held her close, comforting her.

I looked at what remained of the forest around me. Somehow, not all of the trees were dead. Their trunks were charred black, but they still had tufts of green leaves. And while the ground was now barren, I knew that wouldn't be the case for long. Fire was a natural part of the lives of forests. Many plants actually needed the underbrush to be burned away before they would have enough light to grow. Within a few weeks, grasses and flowers would emerge from the baked earth, and over the next few years, the trees and bushes would return. But that was of little solace to someone who'd lost their prized possessions in the fire.

"So?" Summer pressed my parents. "Teddy can come with us, right? It solves all your problems."

"Not exactly *all* of them," Dad corrected, waving to the space where our house had been.

"I mean the short-term ones," Summer said. "Teddy needs a place to stay. So he can stay with us in Malibu. Done."

"Sounds good to me," I said. Despite my home being gone, I was now feeling excited. I had never been to California before, and I'd heard that the beaches in Malibu were amazing.

"You don't have anything to wear," Mom reminded me. "All your clothes are gone."

"We'll get some at FunJungle Emporium before we

leave," Summer assured her. "They sell everything there."

This was true. The Emporium was so big, it had a larger clothing section than most department stores—although every last bit of it was branded with FunJungle logos or characters. Even the boxer shorts.

"Please?" I implored my parents. "Can I go?"

Mom and Dad looked at each other again. Apparently, neither of them could think of a reason to say no. Mom turned back to Summer. "I suppose that if your mother says it's all right, then we'd be okay with it."

Summer beamed. "I know she will! Mom loves Teddy!"

Sure enough, Kandace McCracken was happy to have me join them. Which was how, less than a day later, I found myself at the beach in Malibu, California, staying in the biggest house I had ever been inside.

It was the home of one of Kandace's best friends, a fellow model who went by only one name: Binka. She was originally from Brazil, but she had married an extremely successful land developer named Roswell Crowe. Roswell had become fabulously rich building mansions for celebrities and then decided to top them all when building his own home.

The marriage hadn't worked out. According to Kandace, Binka and Roswell were in the midst of a very nasty divorce. Binka had ended up with the beach house, while Roswell got the mansion in Beverly Hills.

The beach house was extremely modern, with large open spaces and enormous windows facing the Pacific Ocean. My entire home could have fit inside the living room. The house was filled with paintings that I didn't like and expensive furniture that seemed to be designed for looks rather than comfort. Binka eagerly gave us a tour when we arrived, rattling off the names of the creators of each work of art. "That's a Twombly. That's a Haring. And that's a Bartleby-Combs." She pointed lazily around the room as she spoke, so I couldn't tell if she was talking about paintings or furniture. Apparently, I was expected to know the names of everyone she mentioned.

Kandace gasped with delight at everything, while behind their backs, Summer quietly made faces of disgust for my amusement.

As far as I was concerned, the most beautiful thing about the house was the view. Beyond the windows, the Pacific shimmered under a cloudless blue sky, while the beach arced away to either side. The house had a wide raised deck with an infinity pool overlooking the beach. Sliding glass doors led out to it, but for some reason, they were all closed, cutting off the ocean breeze. Without it, the air in the house felt stale—and there was a strange faint smell of decay.

We had come directly to Binka's from the airport. Much of our route had taken us along the Pacific Coast Highway, which followed the shoreline from the more populated section of the city out to Malibu. Flying in, I had been astonished to see how big and spread out Los Angeles was; the last twenty minutes of the flight had been over a continuous stretch of urban sprawl. But there was also a surprising amount of wilderness in the midst of the city. From the plane, I had noted a range of mountains cutting straight through the metropolis. Some of it was developed, but most was open space. That same range continued on into Malibu, running directly along the coast. Much of Malibu was built on the extremely narrow strip of land between the mountains and the beach. In many spots, there was so little room that the houses couldn't quite fit; their fronts were built on solid ground, while their backs perched on stilts over the beach. However, the area where Binka lived was different.

It was called the Colony, and even in Malibu, which was full of wealthy, exclusive neighborhoods, this one was regarded as the wealthiest and most exclusive. It was a gated community of opulent mansions, situated on a wide, flat delta that jutted out into the Pacific from the base of the mountains.

And yet, something struck me as odd about the Colony: almost no one had any sort of yard at all. The mansions were all built on thin strips of land and were so large, they took up almost their entire properties. The whole community was a line of giant beachfront homes wedged together like bricks, with barely any room between them. Binka's mansion was a prime example: it had more rooms than Binka seemed to know what to do with, but not a single square inch of lawn. It was as though she and Roswell hadn't cared at all about being outside—unless it was by the pool.

Binka was rattling off the long list of famous people who were neighbors: movie stars, professional athletes, singers, and people who'd made a killing on the internet. I had known what Binka looked like long before meeting her, as she appeared in the advertisements for dozens of products (including a campaign for FunJungle, which Kandace had recruited her for), and Xavier had most of them taped to the interior of his school locker. But in real life, Binka looked somewhat different: skinnier and more angular. Her skin was so bronzed, it was almost black, though I didn't know if that was the natural color or the result of a serious tanning regimen. She finished her list of famous neighbors with a director whose last four films had been financial disasters. "I hear he's broke and desperate for cash," she told Kandace. "He paid nearly thirty million for his place, but I'll bet you and J.J. could get it for less. And then you could live here by me instead of on that ridiculous dusty ranch in the middle of nowhere."

Beside me, Summer gave a sharp intake of breath, as though afraid that her mother might want to do this.

To her relief—and mine—Kandace declined diplomatically. "As nice as all this is, I *like* my dusty ranch in the middle of nowhere."

"Oh please," Binka said dismissively. "It must be so boring out there, with no one to talk to but horses and cows. And you're destroying your career, being so far off the beaten path. Do you know how I landed the new mascara line from Deluxe?"

Kandace turned to her, surprised. "That's going to be you?"

"I thought you knew!" Binka frowned. "This is exactly what I'm talking about. You don't even know what's going on in our business. I got the gig by just walking on the beach outside my door. I was passing my neighbor's, and he was having a party, so he told me to join him, and the whole patio was chock full of agents. I ended up talking to a few of them over champagne, one said I'd be great for Deluxe, and the next thing I knew, I had the job."

"That's amazing," Kandace said supportively, although I thought I could detect a hint of jealously.

"No," Binka said. "It's not amazing at all. It's how life works out here. If you lived here, *you* would have the Deluxe account instead of me, because you're even more beautiful than I am. . . ."

"That's not true," Kandace said.

"You're right," Binka agreed. "You know who'd have the account? *This* gorgeous creature." She suddenly cupped Summer's face in her hands. "You are ten times more beautiful than both of us!" she exclaimed. "You could be minting money with this gorgeous face! What are you even doing in Texas?"

"Going to school," Summer reminded her. "I'm only fifteen."

"School," Binka spat, in the same tone of disgust that someone else might have said "leeches." "With looks like this, you don't need school. By the time I was your age, I was already making tons of money as a model. So was your mother. And you could too."

"I *like* school," Summer said sharply.

Binka didn't seem to hear this. "There are some people you should meet while you're here. Both of you. I'm going to make some calls."

"That's not necessary . . . ," Kandace began.

"It is. It absolutely is. I'll do it while you get settled in your rooms." Binka paused suddenly, confused. "Wasn't there someone else with you?"

"Doc," Kandace said, looking confused herself. "Where'd he get off to?"

"He had some business to take care of," I told them.

Doc had come with us on the jet and then in the car

from the airport, but had barely said a word the entire time. The moment we had arrived at Binka's house, he had slipped away to use his phone. I got the impression he was in a hurry to make the call but hadn't wanted anyone to overhear it, or else he would have called during the drive.

I was pleased Binka had been distracted from pestering Summer and Kandace to move from Texas to Malibu. Before she could start again, I tried to change the subject permanently. "This is a really great view," I said, pointing out the windows.

"It is," Binka agreed. "That's why we paid a small fortune to live here."

"Could we go out on the deck to get a better look?" I asked, starting for the sliding glass doors.

Binka stepped into my path, blocking me. She now looked somewhat embarrassed. "Normally, I'd say yes. In fact, that would have been the first stop on the tour; seeing the view is really the pièce de résistance. But I'm afraid we need to keep the doors and windows closed for now. Because of the smell."

Now that she'd mentioned it, I noticed the smell of decay again. And it seemed stronger the closer I was to the windows.

Kandace and Summer noticed it too and wrinkled their noses in disgust. "What is that?" Kandace asked. "Did something die?"

"Don't you watch the news?" Binka asked. "Yes, something died. *That*." She pointed through the windows at something down the beach.

"Oh my gosh!" Summer exclaimed. Then, despite Binka's warning and her mother's protests, she opened a sliding door anyhow and ran out onto the pool deck.

The odor was significantly stronger with the door open, although I had encountered worse while living at FunJungle. For example, it wasn't nearly as bad as the accumulated poop of a hundred penguins. So I joined Summer on the deck to get a better look at the source of the smell.

About a hundred yards away, on the sand in front of some of the priciest homes in America, was the thirty-ton corpse of a whale.

THE CARCASS

The blue whale is the largest animal that has ever lived on earth, by far.

Adults can grow up to 110 feet long, which is the length of a commercial airplane, and weigh 170 tons—or about as much as twenty-five full-grown elephants. The tongue alone can weigh six thousand pounds, the same as a hippopotamus. The largest sauropod dinosaurs, the biggest land animals known to science, were only a third of the size of a blue whale. Even other whales, like humpbacks, are dwarfed by blues.

The dead whale on the beach was a juvenile, only about half as big as an adult, but it was staggeringly large.

Most people never get to see an entire whale. Even when you go looking for them on sightseeing boats, you rarely catch more than a fleeting glimpse of the spout or the tail. If you're lucky enough to see one breach, the experience is over within seconds. For the most part, the bulk of the animal is hidden underwater. Now I had the rare chance to see a whale in its entirety—although the circumstances were admittedly sad ones.

The animal appeared to have beached itself and then died; its gigantic head was pointed inland, while its tail remained in the surf. The tide was at its lowest point, meaning the beach was about as wide as it would get, and still, the whale stretched all the way across, a great wall of dead flesh.

The whale was tilted on its right side, so that its belly was aimed toward Binka's house. As with many marine animals, the skin on its underside was significantly lighter than the rest of its body. This was a form of camouflage known as countershading; when you look down into the depths of the ocean, the water is dark, so dark skin blends in when seen from above, whereas when you look up toward the surface, the water is lighter, thanks to the sun, and lighter skin blends in when seen from below.

According to Binka, the whale had already been there for three days, and the neighbors were enraged. They wanted someone to haul it away: the Coast Guard, the police, the navy—they didn't care who. But NOAA, the National Oceanic and Atmospheric Administration, had jurisdiction and wanted to do an autopsy first. "So now, that giant rotting corpse is just lying there, ruining our beach and stinking up our homes," Binka complained.

"I'm sure that NOAA has a good reason for wanting to dissect the whale," Summer said.

"Then why haven't they done it already?" Binka griped. "I'll bet, if these NOAA people had dead whales on their front lawns, they would have them moved in a minute!"

I could understand her frustration. As fascinating as the dead whale was, I probably wouldn't have wanted it in front of my home for a long period of time. (Although I currently had even bigger problems where home was concerned.) The carcass was already decaying, and it seemed to have attracted every seagull in Los Angeles County. Clouds of them swarmed the enormous dead body; the beach around it was spackled white with their poop.

Despite this, I wanted a closer look at the whale. So did Summer—to her mother's dismay. But then, we weren't the only ones who were intrigued. A large crowd of onlookers had come to see the massive corpse.

Binka had explained that all beaches in California were officially public property. So while the Colony had gates to prevent people from approaching their houses by road, anyone was allowed to visit the beach; it just took some work. A public beach called Malibu Lagoon lay a half mile east. Most of the onlookers had walked over from there, although others had come by sea kayak and stand-up paddleboard. The whale had become something of a tourist attraction. People had come from as far away as New Mexico to see it. Binka said that many of the first visitors had climbed on the whale or stolen bits of the carcass, and then posted photos of their exploits on social media. NOAA hadn't been pleased, and so the Los Angeles Sheriff's Department had now cordoned the body off with yellow police tape and posted a deputy on each side to keep the crowds at bay. No one was being allowed within thirty feet of the carcass.

Luckily, Summer and I had a way to get closer.

It turned out Doc knew the scientist from NOAA who was going to perform the autopsy, a whale specialist named Cassandra Carson. Doc claimed she was one of the best in her field. The procedure was going to take place that afternoon, and Doc had asked if he could observe. Dr. Carson had eagerly agreed, thinking it would be helpful to have a renowned vet like Doc on hand. So Summer and I had volunteered to help as well. All we had to do was talk Doc into it.

Although that wasn't so easy.

"We'll behave ourselves," Summer insisted, as we accompanied Doc down the beach on his way to the autopsy. "I promise."

"No," Doc said gruffly. "This is a job for professionals. Not amateurs."

"We'll let you handle all the important stuff," I told him. "And you can have us do all the stuff that you don't want to do."

"Right," Summer agreed. "You can give us the most disgusting jobs. We'll do them without any question at all."

I gave her a sidelong glance, worried she was going too far. I had once witnessed the autopsy of a hippopotamus; there had been plenty of disgusting body parts—and I figured, with a whale, the disgusting body parts might be even bigger than I was. I only wanted to get a better look at the whale, not end up holding a jumbo-size gallbladder.

Doc paused before answering, seeming slightly pleased by the idea of making Summer and me do something really repulsive, but then he thought better of it and shook his head. "It was hard enough for *me* to get permission to participate. I can't ask to bring children along."

"We're not *children*," Summer said, sounding offended. "We're teenagers. And, in case you've forgotten, we've been awfully good at solving crimes."

"This isn't a crime," Doc huffed. "No one murdered this whale. It's not like we're going to find stab wounds or a giant martini glass with a residue of arsenic."

"Then why even do an autopsy?" I asked.

"To determine the cause of death, obviously."

"You just said it wasn't a crime!" Summer exclaimed.

"Yes. But there may have been environmental factors that led to the whale's death. If we can determine what those are, then maybe we can prevent more cetaceans from dying."

"If the whale died due to environmental factors, that sure sounds like a crime to me," Summer muttered under her breath.

We were still fifty yards away from the whale, but the smell had become significantly worse. Now that we were closing in, the astonishing size of the beast was becoming more and more evident. It felt like we were approaching a building, rather than an animal. The carcass was nearly the size of my mobile home. Even the tallest onlookers were dwarfed by it.

I was now getting a better look at the condition of the carcass as well. From a distance, it had appeared to be in decent shape, as if it had been embalmed by an enormous coroner. But from closer, I could see that it had begun to decompose. There were many gashes in the skin, revealing the dark flesh beneath, although I couldn't tell if those were a result of the decaying process or the horde of seagulls pecking at the corpse. It was probably a bit of both. The portion of the body that was still in the ocean had suffered the most; much of the tail was missing.

I pointed to it. "What happened there?"

"Sharks, I'd bet," Doc replied. "Hammerheads, great whites, and plenty of other species live off this coast. When the tide's in, the water must be several feet higher." He pointed to the homes we were passing.

Instead of being situated directly on the beach, all the mansions were raised up a story, atop ten-foot seawalls, just as Binka's had been. This meant that each required a wooden staircase to get to the beach, although, due to erosion, no one's stairs reached all the way to the sand anymore; the bottom steps all dangled a foot above the ground. (The situation had been even worse at Binka's, where a three-foot gap between her stairs and the sand had required temporarily duct-taping a stepladder in place for beach access.) I noted that the lowest third of the concrete seawalls was slightly darker than the rest, indicating how high the tide could reach.

"In water that deep, there's plenty of room for sharks to move around," Doc observed.

"They'll come that close to the shore?" I asked.

"If there's food around, a shark will practically beach itself to get to it." Doc stared at the water around the remains of the dead whale's tail. "In fact, there's probably some lurking out there right now."

I clutched Summer's hand, worried. Even though I knew shark attacks on humans were extremely rare, they were certainly much more likely in an area where sharks were feeding. "Maybe helping out with this autopsy isn't such a good idea," I said.

She gave me a look of surprise. "You don't want to see what the whale looks like on the inside?"

"Er . . . not really."

Summer frowned as though I had just refused to go to a theme park. Before she could argue, though, Cassandra Carson emerged from the crowd of onlookers.

We had just arrived at the point where the sheriff's department had strung the line of yellow crime scene tape, thirty feet from the carcass. One end of the tape was tied to a wooden staircase at the seawall, while the other was tied to a metal pole that had been jabbed in the sand. The public beach was on the opposite side of the whale from us, so the crowd on that side was larger, but there was still a good number of people who had braved the potentially sharky waters and waded around the tail to visit our side. The deputy who had been posted there was dutifully patrolling the line, doing his best to look imposing, despite the fact that he was wearing swimmer's nose plugs. I presumed they were to keep him from smelling the whale; now that I was so close, I wished I had a pair myself. The stench of the carcass and all the seagulls was enough to make me reel.

Dr. Carson didn't seem to be affected by the smell at all.

In fact, she was in an exceptionally good mood for someone who was about to autopsy a gigantic corpse. She had the broad-shouldered build of an athlete, and her long hair was pulled back into a ponytail. Despite the sunny day, she wore a heavy hazmat suit over her clothes—and she was carrying what looked like the world's biggest scalpel: a two-foot blade of steel at the end of a long metal pole. She greeted Doc with a big smile. "Freakin' Deakin! It's about time you got here! Any longer and the seagulls would have eaten it all."

Doc smiled in response. "It's nice to see you, too, Cass."

Summer and I shared a look of surprise. Seeing Doc smile and say it was nice to see someone was even more astonishing than encountering a dead whale on the beach.

Cass glanced at us, then back to Doc. "I didn't realize you'd be bringing the kids."

Doc flushed red. "These aren't my kids," he said quickly. "And I was just explaining to them that they *couldn't* come."

Cass laughed at his reaction and held up an open palm, signaling he could calm down. "Relax. I'm just joking. I know you're too old for kids this age." She flashed him a taunting grin.

Summer grinned as well, amused. "I'm Summer McCracken. And this is Teddy Fitzroy. We help Doc with his work all the time."

"They do not," Doc declared.

"It's nice to meet you, Dr. Carson," I said.

"Please, call me Cass. 'Doctor' is way too formal for me. Unlike some people I could name." She nodded toward Doc and grinned once more.

To my astonishment, Doc laughed in response.

I pointed to the giant blade Cass was holding. "What's that?"

"This is a flensing knife." Cass held it out so we could get a better look. "Whalers use them to cut through the skin and remove the blubber. They also come in handy for autopsies. Sad to say, some countries still haven't outlawed whaling yet, so people are continuing to make these tools, which is why this one's relatively new and not an antique. Although, it's not like every NOAA office has one of these bad boys. This had to be brought down from San Francisco, which is why I didn't do this autopsy two days ago."

"You weren't just waiting for Doc to show up?" Summer asked teasingly.

"Well, I'm happy to have the extra hands," Cass said. "For some reason, the rest of the folks in my office didn't relish the idea of spending a hot summer afternoon poking around inside a rotting whale."

"If you need extra hands, Teddy and I can help too!" Summer proclaimed.

I grimaced. The more I thought about it, the less I liked the idea of helping with the autopsy.

"That'd be great," Cass said. "Although, for safety reasons, I can't let either of you inside the whale."

"Oh darn," I said sarcastically—although Summer looked genuinely upset. "Really?" she asked.

"Trust me, you don't want to go in there if you don't have to," Cass assured her, then got down to business. "Now, what we have here is a juvenile blue whale, age approximately three to five years old, cause of death undetermined—so far."

"How do you know its age?" I asked. "Just from its size?"

"Partially," Cass replied. "A blue whale reaches maturity at only ten years old, despite the fact that they can live to almost a hundred. A newborn can be twenty-five feet long and three tons—and they grow incredibly fast. In their first year, drinking nothing but milk, they gain two hundred pounds a day."

"Holy cow," I said.

Cass grinned, appreciating our attention. "But if we really want to get the age of a whale right, especially the older ones, you know what we do?"

"Check their ID?" Doc asked.

Cass gave a snort of laughter. "No. We examine their earwax."

That seemed almost as ridiculous an answer as Doc's. "No way," Summer said.

"Whales are all evolved from animals that used to live on land," Cass explained. "So they still have remnants from that time on their bodies. For example, most whales have vestigial leg bones near their pelvises, which don't do anything anymore, except prove that they used to have hind legs. And they also have earholes, which are left over from when they had external ears. Those don't do anything either, except collect earwax, which must be really annoying for whales, since they don't have fingers to clean them out."

"Or enormous Q-tips," Doc said, provoking another laugh from Cass.

Summer turned to me, amused, then whispered, "Doc's telling jokes?"

"I know," I whispered back, equally astonished. "I thought he was born without a funny bone."

"So here's what we need to do . . . ," Cass began—but before she could get any further, a surfer interrupted her.

His skin was so weathered and wrinkled from the sun that it was hard to guess how old he was; he might have been an old man who was in surprisingly good shape as a result of all the surfing he'd done—or he might have been a young man who was in extremely *bad* shape due to all the surfing. His hair was long, wet, and stringy. He wore a neoprene wet suit that had been patched repeatedly and carried a surfboard that had obviously been lovingly cared for. But there was something off about him; his eyes were slightly glazed, and he had the tone of voice of someone who was perpetually confused.

"Hey!" he said to Cass. "You're here from the government, right?"

"That's right," Cass agreed.

"Are you here to investigate the beach that's been stolen?"

Cass gave the surfer a wary look. "Er . . . no. I'm here to autopsy the whale."

The surfer frowned, disappointed. "Really?"

"Really. That's why I'm carrying this giant knife and standing next to the carcass."

"Oh. 'Cause I've been calling the government for the past three days about the stolen beach, and no one's come out to investigate it yet. Which branch of the government are you with?"

"NOAA," Cass said, obviously wanting to end this conversation quickly. "And I really need to get this autopsy started. . . ."

"I called NOAA!" the surfer exclaimed. "And also the police, the FBI, the Coast Guard, the navy, the Fish and Wildlife Service, the fire department, the Bureau of Sanitation—"

"Sanitation?" Summer interrupted. "Why?"

"I was trying to get anyone who would answer the

phone," the surfer replied, then told Cass, "This is a huge deal and you need to look into it."

"This is a pretty big deal too," I said, pointing at the dead whale behind us, trying to help Cass. "In fact, it's *enormous*."

"What do you mean someone stole the beach?" Summer asked the surfer, obviously intrigued by him. "Doesn't look like it's been stolen to me."

"Not *this* beach," the surfer replied, like maybe Summer was the one who wasn't making sense. He pointed toward the public beach on the other side of the dead whale. "The one down there, by the lagoon. Three nights ago, a huge part of it just vanished. It was there at sunset, but in the morning, it was gone."

"Part of the beach vanished?" Summer repeated, trying to understand.

While she was distracting the surfer, Cass took a few steps back, attempting to slip away.

"Yeah, like a whole bunch of sand," the surfer said. "Tons of it."

"It was probably just the tide," Summer suggested.

The surfer shook his head. "No way. I've surfed that beach almost every day for over thirty years. I know how the tides work. This wasn't normal. The sand didn't just wash away. Someone *stole* it." He suddenly wheeled on Cass, freezing her in her tracks. "You have to do something about this!"

Cass looked to Doc, obviously hoping he would get her out of this.

And to my surprise, he did. He turned to the surfer and acted nice and friendly.

"I appreciate you bringing this to our attention," he said, then lowered his voice to a conspiratorial whisper. "The fact is, we're not here to dissect this whale at all. We're with the FBI's beach protection division. This is an undercover operation to investigate the theft of that sand."

"No way!" the surfer exclaimed.

"Shhhh!" Doc hissed. "Don't give us away! The sand thieves might very well be here right now."

The surfer looked warily at the crowd of onlookers, then grew worried. "You think they've returned to the scene of the crime?"

"It happens all the time," Doc told him. "Now, for your own protection, I need you to leave us to handle this. And don't say another word about this to anyone—or you could end up dead."

The surfer's eyes went wide, but then he nodded. "All right. My name's Dave, by the way. Although everyone calls me Sharky. In case you need any more help."

"We don't," Doc said. "You've done more than enough by bringing this case to our attention. The FBI thanks you. Now just move along and let us take care of this."

"All right." Sharky saluted, then headed back into the water with his surfboard, apparently not concerned about sharks—or dead whale bits—in the slightest.

The moment he was out of earshot, Cass broke into a fit of giggles, then looked to Doc with wonder. "That was brilliant! He totally bought it! I didn't know you could act like that!"

"Neither did *we*," Summer said, staring at Doc with surprise.

Cass returned her attention to the whale. "Okay," she told us. "Let's get to work." She was about to slip under the cordon of police tape when yet another man approached us.

He appeared to be in his early twenties and was strikingly handsome, with perfectly coiffed hair and gleaming teeth. He looked as though he had just stepped off the cover of a magazine, and came toward us from the direction of the whale's head, well inside the cordoned-off area.

"Hey!" the deputy shouted at him. "You're not supposed to be on that side of the tape!"

"I'm terribly sorry," the man replied in a very charming manner. "But you see, my home is on *this* side of the tape. It's that one right there." He pointed to the house that was closest to the head of the whale, a massive mansion that was designed to look like a French château.

To me, the man seemed surprisingly young to be able to

afford such a huge house on an exclusive stretch of beach. Although even more surprising was the way that everyone reacted to him. The deputy immediately backed down, obviously embarrassed about the way he had spoken to him, while the crowd of onlookers murmured excitedly.

But the *most* unusual thing about the man was Summer's reaction to him. She gaped in astonishment as he came toward us. Her usual cool demeanor vanished, and she became downright giddy. "Oh my gosh," she squealed. "You're Jackson Cross!"

The man flashed her a dynamite smile. "That's right. And you are . . . ?"

"Summer. *Space Cadets* was my favorite TV show *ever*!"

Now I understood who the man was—and why he was so wealthy. As a child, he had been the star of several TV shows, including *Space Cadets*, which was about the adventures of a group of kids who lived on an intergalactic spaceship. According to Summer, the show had been immensely popular, but I had missed it—along with just about all other pop culture—as I had been living in the jungle in the Congo. I recalled Summer saying that Jackson Cross had also been in some hit films as a child, but I'd never seen any of those, either.

It was obvious that he was used to being recognized; everyone else on the beach seemed to know who he was, and several were holding out scraps of paper and pens to get his signature. But he appeared genuinely flattered by Summer's praise. "That's very kind of you to say. I'm just sorry that we had to meet under such"—he cast a sidelong glance at the dead whale—"unfortunate circumstances."

"Not at all," Summer said. "I think the whale's kind of cool."

"I suppose it is, in a way," Jackson said gamely, although I got the sense he didn't think the giant carcass was cool at all. "Or, at least, it was on the first day." He shifted his attention to Cass. "But now it's *day three*. And my neighbors and I are all wondering why it's still here." He waved grandly toward the other mansions.

Several of the homeowners were standing at the railings of their pool decks, watching this exchange from a distance. It appeared as though Jackson Cross had been selected to speak for all of them, perhaps with the idea that his star power would have the same effect on Cass that it did on Summer.

It didn't. Cass didn't seem the slightest bit impressed by the actor. "We're working on it," she informed him. "As you can see, we're about to perform the autopsy. Once the cause of death has been determined, we'll see about having the body removed."

Jackson's smile twitched, as though it was trying to

become a frown. "I'm afraid that's unacceptable. My neighbors and I feel that we have already suffered enough due to this festering monstrosity. We want it moved as soon as possible."

"I understand that this is an inconvenience . . . ," Cass began diplomatically.

"An inconvenience?" Jackson scoffed. "No. An inconvenience is traffic on the coast highway. Or sand in your shoe. This whale is a catastrophe! It's ugly, it's disgusting, and, as I'm sure you've noticed, the smell is ungodly."

Once again, Cass looked to Doc for help. And once again, he came to her rescue. "Mr. Cross, every minute you spend haranguing us is another minute that we're not working on the autopsy. Holding us up is only going to make things worse. . . ."

"Worse?" Jackson echoed, his bearing really starting to crack. "There's a gigantic corpse right under my infinity pool, every inch of my house smells like rotting fish, and there's a million seagulls crapping on my deck! How could things possibly get worse?"

At that very moment, the dead whale exploded.

THE EXPLOSION

Bizarrely, this was not my first time seeing a large, dead animal explode.

A year earlier, I had been in attendance when the bloated corpse of Henry the Hippo was accidentally dropped from a great height during his funeral at FunJungle. That had been a supremely disgusting experience.

This was much, much worse.

For starters, the corpse in question was significantly larger. Henry had been a plus-size hippopotamus, but even then, he maxed out at two tons. The juvenile whale weighed fifteen times more than that.

And in this case, someone had blown up the dead body on purpose.

It was obvious, right from the very first moment, that

explosives were involved. A *lot* of explosives. An enormous blast tore the corpse apart with such force that everyone in the vicinity was knocked off our feet, even though we were all ten yards away. The carcass was instantly reduced to millions of pieces, which flew through the air and rained down over some of the most expensive real estate on earth. Most of the pieces were very small, mere flecks of flesh or blubber, but there were quite a few larger bits that caused a considerable amount of damage.

A shard of rib the size of a full-grown elephant's tusk smashed through the plate glass window of one nearby mansion and speared a grand piano. A thirty-pound chunk of liver cannonballed into another home hard enough to punch a hole in the roof. A six-foot-long strip of blubber somehow sailed a quarter of a mile and flattened a brandnew Lamborghini.

Jackson Cross's home got the worst of it, though. His mansion had a wide expanse of windows facing the ocean. The shock wave of the blast shattered them, leaving the interior of the house exposed to the surge of viscera that followed. His walls, floors, and art were doused by a deluge of whale gunk. His infinity pool turned so red, it looked like an enormous bowl of minestrone soup.

I staggered back to my feet, my ears ringing from the explosion. All around me, the beach—and the people on it—was dappled with red goo, but thankfully, everyone seemed to be unharmed.

The same couldn't be said for the seagulls. Most of the flock had been decimated by the blast. All that was left were thousands of feathers, which now wafted down from the sky like snowflakes. However, for the lucky gulls that had survived, the entire beach had been turned into a massive buffet. They swarmed the sand, gorging themselves.

The explosion had vaporized the central two thirds of the whale. Part of its head and a good section of its tail remained on the beach, but the rest was gone, as though the biggest carnivore in the universe had taken a bite out of it. Some of the whale had been blown so high that tiny bits were still plunking down around us.

"My house!" Jackson Cross shrieked. "My beautiful house!" He was so upset, he didn't even seem to notice he was covered in whale guts and bolted back across the sand to confront the damage.

Meanwhile, I was *very* aware of all the whale guts on me. My arms, legs, and shirt were covered with it, and I could sense it was also in my hair. I quickly tried to wipe as much off as possible with my hands.

Beside me, Summer was doing the same thing. "This . . . is . . . disgusting," she groaned, flicking miscellaneous whale bits off her arms.

Nearby, Doc helped Cass to her feet. She looked bewildered. "Wh-what just happened?" she stammered.

"Someone blew up that whale," Doc said. He was as angry as I'd ever seen him—and Doc was angry a lot.

The statement only seemed to confuse Cass more. She looked to Doc as though perhaps she hadn't heard him right. Which was understandable. My hearing had definitely been affected by the blast. Everyone's words were muted, as though I were hearing them underwater.

"Why?" Cass asked.

"I don't know," Doc replied. "But maybe we can find out." He scanned the beach around the blast zone.

There was a good-size gob of blubber stuck in his mustache, making it look like he had a severely runny nose, but he was in such a foul mood, I didn't want to tell him.

By the seawall, Jackson Cross clambered up the blubber-slicked staircase to his pool deck—and then screamed with renewed horror upon seeing the wreckage of his home. "My kitchen! My breakfast nook! My Picasso!"

Cass came to Doc's side. "What are you looking for?"

"Whoever set those explosives off is probably still close by." Doc continued scanning the beach.

I did too. So did Summer. "How will we recognize them?" she asked.

"They won't look like everyone else," Doc replied. "This wasn't a surprise to them."

I still didn't know quite what Doc meant—until I saw the two guys.

They were on what had been the opposite side of the whale. A minute before, there had been a wall of dead animal in between us, but now it was gone, so we had a perfectly good view of them.

Everyone else on the beach was still recovering from the shock of the explosion. Many were sitting on the sand, trying to comprehend what had happened. Others were frantically wiping dead whale off themselves. Two bikini-clad women were clambering out of the pool next door to Jackson Cross, wailing in disgust.

Meanwhile, the two guys I'd spotted were laughing. They had been standing well behind the other onlookers, probably thinking they were far enough to avoid being hit by any remains. They weren't—but they definitely had avoided the worst of it. They looked college-aged and were dressed similarly, in board shorts, T-shirts, and baseball caps. To them, the aftermath of the explosion was hilarious.

One was laughing so hard, he was doubled over. The other was giggling nervously, like a kid who had just hit a baseball through the neighbor's window.

"There!" I exclaimed, pointing at them.

Doc saw them and his gaze hardened. He turned to the sheriff's deputy who had been stationed on our side of the whale. He was still gawking at what remained of the carcass, eyes wide in shock. "Hey!" Doc yelled, then pointed to the college guys as well. "I think those kids were behind this!"

The college guys both stopped laughing. The one who'd been doubled over straightened up, eyes wide. The one who'd been giggling started to back away, trying his best to look innocent, but failing.

The deputy didn't do anything. He was so shell-shocked, he might not have even heard Doc. But Cass leaped into action. She sprinted down the beach toward the college guys, still clutching her flensing knife.

It was my guess that Cass had forgotten she was even holding the giant blade, although it was possible that she wanted the boys to think she intended to use it. Whatever the case, it scared the pants off them. Both turned and bolted down the beach.

Doc and Summer raced after Cass, and, without even thinking about it, I joined them.

The shortest path to the college guys took us directly through what remained of the whale. Besides the head and tail, there wasn't much; most of the body had been blown elsewhere—although the explosion had left a crater in the sand that we had to pass through. It barely slowed Cass at all. She was in exceptionally good shape and full of determination. Even with the flensing knife, she tore across the sand.

Both of the college guys had the muscular builds of people who spent a lot of time in the gym, but all their bulk made them slower than Cass. The one who'd been doubled over was slightly bigger and faster, though. He was leaving his friend behind.

"Wait!" the smaller guy shouted. "Don't leave me!"

The bigger one didn't listen. He didn't even look back. There was something clutched in his hand, and, as he ran, he tried to get rid of it. He twisted sideways in midstride and flung it toward the ocean. However, in doing so, he took his eyes off where he was heading.

A large, ragged strip of whale skin lay on the sand in front of him, blubber side up. Blubber looks a lot like fat, but it is really a different substance. Fat is used to store energy, whereas blubber is designed to keep marine animals warm in cold water. Because of this, the blubber layer can be up to a foot thick; a single blue whale can produce fifty tons of it. The piece lying in front of the college guy was about two feet square and eight inches deep—and, like fat, it was extremely slippery. The guy stepped on it, and his feet skidded right out from under him. He flopped onto his back atop the blubber with a wet thwack, landing so hard that the wind was knocked out of him.

His friend, who he'd been about to leave behind, now

ditched him. He ran right past his fallen buddy and sprinted on down the beach.

Doc directed Summer and me to the ocean as we ran. "See if you can find what he threw in there! We'll take care of him!"

I knew better than to question Doc's orders when he was in a bad mood. Summer and I veered into the surf while Doc and Cass continued toward the fallen college guy.

Since the tide was at its lowest point, there was a wide stretch of very shallow water along the beach. Even though the college guy was big and strong, he hadn't been able to throw his evidence all the way across it.

"There!" Summer shouted, pointing.

The object the guy had thrown was tumbling in the surf close to the shoreline, although the current was about to drag it out to sea.

Summer and I raced through the shallow water, hoping to get to the mysterious object before that happened. Otherwise, it might vanish into the sea forever. The surf was full of whale bits; tiny pieces of blubber bobbed about everywhere like tiny icebergs. We scattered a small flock of seagulls that was gulping them down. The object disappeared under the surf just before we reached it. I plunged into the deeper water and rooted around desperately. Something long and skinny grazed my hand. I grabbed on tight and lifted it out.

I was clutching the antenna of a small plastic device. It looked like the back half of a gun, with a handgrip and a trigger, and was made of dark plastic.

Summer stopped in the surf beside me, staring at it. "What is that?"

"I think it's a remote detonator," I answered. "Guess we've got the right guys."

A shark fin sliced through the water nearby. It was only a few inches across, meaning the shark was too small to eat me, but it gave me the shivers anyhow. I grabbed Summer's hand, and we hurried back out of the water.

Doc and Cass were now standing over the college guy who had slipped on the blubber. His friend had escaped down the beach, but Cass had ensured that this guy wasn't going anywhere. She held the flensing knife like a spear, the blade aimed at his belly, holding him at bay.

The guy was being cocky and belligerent. "Put the knife down, lady! I'm just an innocent bystander! My father's one of the biggest lawyers in LA. If you so much as nick me with that, he'll sue you for everything you own!"

Summer grabbed the detonator from me and dangled it in his face. "If you're so innocent, what were you doing with this?"

The college guy gulped, obviously surprised that we had recovered the evidence. "I've never seen that before," he said weakly.

"We just saw you throw it into the ocean, you moron," Cass snapped.

"I'm no moron," college guy said defensively. "I'm in my second year at Harvard!"

"Well I don't think you'll be going back," Doc warned menacingly. "You just committed multiple felonies. I don't think Harvard likes having criminals as students."

The college guy grew very concerned as this sank in. He suddenly became much less antagonistic and far more weaselly. "This wasn't my idea! I was tricked into doing it!"

"By who?" Cass held the flensing blade dangerously close to the guy's belly button.

"Some woman I met at a party last night! Sadie—or Zadie—or something like that. This was all her idea!"

A pickup truck came along the beach. It was marked LOS ANGELES COUNTY LIFEGUARD SEARCH AND RESCUE on both sides. Two lifeguards were in the cab. A man who looked to be in his fifties was at the wheel, while a much younger woman sat beside him. They had obviously come from the public beach, most likely in response to the explosion, but now they seemed more concerned about Cass. There was a speaker system attached to the truck, through which the younger lifeguard announced, "Step back from that man and put the spear down!"

Cass shot the lifeguards a look of betrayal. She stepped

back, then held up the flensing knife. "This isn't a spear!" she yelled as the lifeguards parked nearby. "I'm from NOAA, and this is a tool for dissection!"

Summer pointed accusingly at the college guy. "He's the one who blew up the whale! We caught him red-handed!"

"Here's the detonator!" I said helpfully, holding it up. "He threw it in the ocean, but we got it back!"

Now that Cass wasn't looming over him anymore, the guy scuttled away from her and got back to his feet. "That's not *my* detonator!" he proclaimed to everyone at once. "The woman at the party gave it to me! And the dynamite, too!"

"Dynamite?" The older lifeguard was now climbing out of the truck and seeing the results of the explosion up close for the first time. There was a lot to take in; he and the younger lifeguard appeared stunned by the extent of the carnage. The man finally turned his attention back to the college guy and said, "Chase, what have you gotten yourself into this time?"

Even if the lifeguard hadn't called Chase by his name, it was evident from his tone that they knew each other well. I got the sense that they had a long history—and that the lifeguard hadn't enjoyed most of it.

"This wasn't my fault!" Chase protested. "I'm an innocent pawn!"

"We'll see what the sheriff has to say about that. Get in the truck."

Chase stood his ground. "My father's not going to like how you're treating me."

The lifeguard's stare grew several degrees colder. "I said get in the truck, Chase. Are you gonna do that—or do I have to cuff you in front of all of Malibu?" He pointed down the beach.

I had been too focused on Chase to notice until then, but we had drawn a lot of attention. We were far enough from the point of the explosion that the mansions hadn't been too badly slimed with whale guts, although they had still been slightly sullied—and many had cracked windows from the blast. The owners had emerged onto their pool decks to assess the damage, and now they were watching us intently.

Chase didn't say another word. His shoulders slumped like those of a cowering dog, and he trudged across the beach to the truck.

"Skip! Is he the one who blew up the whale?" a middle-aged woman with bleached-blond hair shouted to the lifeguard from her pool deck.

"I don't know, Nancy," the lifeguard replied.

"Well I've got cracks in all my windows and what looks like whale vomit smeared all over my deck," Nancy said angrily. "This is imported mahogany and it's worth a fortune. If it's ruined, that kid's gonna pay."

"That's an issue for you and the sheriff's department," the lifeguard informed her, then turned his attention to Cass and Doc. "I'm Skip Howell. This is quite a mess we've got here. Are both of you with NOAA?"

"Just me," Cass said. "This is Ed Deakin, head veterinarian at FunJungle."

Skip arched an eyebrow, surprised. "FunJungle? You're pretty far from home."

I was also surprised, but for an entirely different reason. I had known Doc for well over a year and never heard anyone call him by his real name. In fact, until that moment, I hadn't even known what his real name *was*.

"I'm on vacation," Doc replied.

"Not much of one," Skip observed. "I take it that all of you witnessed this"—he paused to search for the right words—"unfortunate incident. Including Chase's alleged participation in it?"

"That's right," Summer said.

"Then I'm sure the police will want to talk to all of you as well." Skip cocked his head, listening. The sound of sirens could be heard in the distance. "That's probably them now. Don't go anywhere." With that, he turned away from us.

More lifeguards were arriving in other pickups. Skip started giving them orders.

Doc looked at me and sighed. "What is it with you,

Teddy? You haven't even been in Malibu an hour, and you're already involved in another crime."

"I don't ask for this to happen," I told him. "It just does."

"This isn't going to affect our vacation," Summer assured me. "There's nothing to solve this time." She pointed at Chase, who was sulking in the back of the pickup truck. "That jerk did it. We caught him. Case is closed, pure and simple."

"No, it isn't," Doc said.

Summer and I turned to him, stunned. "You think that guy's really telling the truth?" Summer asked. "You honestly think he was framed?"

"Do you have any idea how much explosive it would take to do that to a blue whale?" Doc nodded back down the beach, to the remnants of the carcass. "That's no college prank. That's a professional job. Someone wanted to get rid of that whale before we did the autopsy. And they found a patsy to pin the blame on."

"But why would someone do that?" I asked.

"I don't know," Doc answered. "But I intend to find out."

QUESTIONS

Even though Malibu felt like a small beach com-
munity, it was part of the city of Los Angeles. Law enforcement was provided by the closest sheriff's department, which was based fifteen miles away over a windy mountain road. A dozen cars had been dispatched in response to the news that there had been a large explosion. The police were stunned by the sight of the decimated whale, but pleased to discover that an obvious suspect had already been apprehended. Since no one wanted to drag us all the way back to the sheriff's department, our statements were taken right on the beach.

I was assigned to Officer Gomez, who was so young, it looked as though he hadn't even started shaving yet. He took down my name and phone number on a small notepad with a stubby pencil. Then he quickly rattled off his questions, as though he really wanted to be doing something else, and showed no patience when I tried to raise questions of my own.

"Did you witness the suspect with the detonator?"

"Yes. Although I didn't actually see him use it. So it's possible that—"

"Did you personally see him throw the detonator in the ocean in an attempt to get rid of the evidence?"

"Well, I saw him throw it, but—"

"Is the suspect on the beach right now?"

"Yes." Three deputies were gathered around Skip's truck, grilling Chase, who looked like he was going to cry.

"Can you identify the suspect for me?"

I pointed to Chase. "That's him, but there was someone else with him."

"Would you be able to recognize that person if you saw them again?"

"Maybe. You should know, there might have been a third person involved. Doc thinks Chase is telling the truth about being set up."

Officer Gomez gave a short laugh. "Do you or Doc have any proof of this? Or is it just speculation?"

"Well, Doc says this explosion looks like the work of a professional, not some college kids."

"Is Doc an expert in explosives or munitions?"

"Er . . . no. He's a veterinarian."

Another short laugh. "Like for dogs and cats?"

"No. At a zoo. He works with all sorts of animals. Elephants and giraffes and lions and such."

"Does he work with whales?"

"There aren't any whales at the zoo. But Doc's really smart. He knows about plenty besides animals. So I think he could be right. What if someone tricked Chase into getting involved in this to set him up?"

This time, the laugh went on a little longer. "Did you see this mystery person out on the beach with Chase and his accomplice?"

"No. But if they were really setting him up, then they probably wouldn't have been here. Or at least not close by . . ."

"You realize how ridiculous this sounds, right?"

I frowned. Now that Officer Gomez had called me on it, it did sound far-fetched. I still pushed on, though. "The person's name is Sadie. Or Zadie."

"How do you know that?"

"Chase told us."

"So, the only way you've ever heard of this mystery person is when the main suspect claimed she existed while professing his innocence?"

"Yes, but—"

"Thanks very much for your time." Officer Gomez closed his notepad. Short of my name and phone number, he hadn't written down one word I'd said. "If we need anything else from you, we'll be in touch." He turned away from me and went to speak to his superior officer.

Summer had had almost the exact same experience with her interview. She couldn't get her officer to take her seriously. Doc's interview had gone slightly differently, but only because he hadn't bothered sharing his theory about the crime at all.

"There wasn't any point," he explained as we walked back along the beach to Binka's house. "As far as the police are concerned, this case is already solved. We gave them a prime suspect and all the evidence they need. The last thing they want is to complicate things for themselves."

Cass had stayed behind with the sheriff's department, which had asked for NOAA's help in coordinating the removal of the whale and cleaning up the beach. The officers had their hands full dealing with all the damage from the explosion. There were dozens of angry millionaires who all wanted their attention at once. Doc had volunteered to stay and help, but a deputy had curtly informed him that his services would not be needed.

The way he'd been treated left Doc in an even more crotchety mood than usual, although it seemed to me that something else might also be upsetting him. He remained sullenly quiet for the rest of our walk.

Binka's mansion was far enough from the exploded carcass that it hadn't sustained much damage, but there were still miscellaneous whale chunks plastered to her windows and floating in her pool. Binka had put both of her full-time maids and her personal chef to work cleaning it up, as well as a man from the pool service. She was overseeing them with a cocktail in one hand and her cell phone in the other.

She wrapped up her call as we climbed the steps to the pool deck. "Thank goodness you're here," she said to Doc. "Do you have any idea what that is?" She pointed to a large, gelatinous piece of whale that was bobbing in her pool.

Doc considered it thoughtfully. "Looks like part of an organ. Maybe the spleen?"

Binka gave him a disappointed look. "You don't know for sure?"

Doc said, "Usually when I see the organs, they're still inside the animals. And in one piece."

"Is it toxic?" Binka asked. "Do I have to drain the pool?"

I considered the pool. So many strange objects were bobbing up and down in it, it looked like an enormous lava lamp.

"I'd drain the pool," Doc said. "And sterilize it too."

Binka sighed heavily, then turned to the pool guy, who

was cautiously prodding a floating lump of goo with a skimmer. "You heard the man. Let's do this."

"Yes, ma'am," the pool guy said, and hurried off to where the pumps were housed.

Doc went to the railing of the deck and stared down the beach, toward the remains of the whale, lost in thought.

Out in the ocean, dozens of dolphins were darting about, their dorsal fins slicing through the surface of the water. The whale carcass was basically chum, and it had attracted plenty of fish, which had then attracted larger predators. I figured there were plenty of sharks out there as well, and made a note not to venture into the ocean for the next few days.

"Where's my mom?" Summer asked.

"In the bathroom," Binka reported. "The sight of all these innards made her sick. And the smell, too. She's been in there ever since the whale blew."

"I should have figured," Summer said.

I should have too. Kandace McCracken had a notoriously weak stomach. I once saw her get nauseated at the sight of bird poop on her car. Whale guts strewn over the deck would probably put her out of commission for the rest of the night.

"You ought to shower before you see her," Binka informed Summer. "You've got whale all over you. And . . ." She sniffed the air and wrinkled her nose. "No offense, but . . . you smell."

We had both done our best to wipe off as much of the whale as possible, but we hadn't been able to get all of it. Summer sniffed a bit on her arm, then recoiled in shock. "Yeah. I could use a shower."

Binka pointed around the edge of the house, the opposite way that the pool guy had gone. "I have an outdoor shower over there. I think it'd be best if all of you use that before coming inside."

I picked a piece of blubber off my shoulder and gave it a tentative sniff. It was absolutely vile. We had simply been surrounded by so much foul-smelling stuff that day that I had stopped noticing it.

"Is it true that Chase Buckingham blew up that whale?" Binka asked.

"How'd you hear that already?" I said.

"This is a small community, darling. And the number one sport here isn't surfing. It's gossip. This is all anyone will be talking about for weeks."

"Chase was definitely involved," said Summer. "We caught him red-handed. Do you know him?"

"I know his father," Binka replied. "He's a real piece of work. One of the biggest corporate lawyers in the state. I haven't gotten to know his new wife yet, but there's not much point. She probably won't last much longer than any of the others."

"How many have there been?" I asked.

"I think this is number six. But maybe it's seven. What's amazing is that Neil Buckingham can keep finding people willing to marry him. But then, I guess having a few hundred million dollars helps."

I noted the irony in these words being spoken by a woman who'd married a wealthy man twenty years older than her.

Then it occurred to me that Binka might have some answers we needed.

"Chase wasn't acting alone," I said. "He was with another kid about his age who got away. They seemed to be friends."

"Was he built just like Chase?" Binka asked, "But a few inches shorter?"

"Yes," Summer answered.

Binka nodded knowingly. "Scooter Derman. Not surprising. Those two are practically connected at the hip. They're even roommates at Harvard."

"What's Scooter's real name?" I asked.

Binka started to answer, then paused. "I have no idea. I've never heard anyone call him anything but Scooter. Even his parents. Who, by the way, are even more loaded than the Buckinghams. Or the Queen of England, for that matter."

A loud hum came from around the side of the house. The pool pump had been turned on to drain the water. There was a gurgling noise, and some large air bubbles blorped up from the drain at the bottom of the pool.

"Do you know where Scooter lives?" Doc asked, so suddenly that it caught all of us by surprise. I hadn't even realized he'd been paying attention.

"They have a house down the beach," Binka said. "Although if Scooter thinks he's in trouble, I doubt he'd go there now. Not with all these police around. He probably went to his family's home in Bel Air. It's about twenty miles from here."

"They have another house that close to this one?" I asked, surprised.

Binka laughed. "Half the homes in the Colony are second homes. If not third or fourth ones. The Dermans have more than I can count—although the Bel Air one is really something. I've been to a few parties there. It's so big, they have servants whose job is solely to take guests to the bathroom, because otherwise they'll get lost."

"So you know Scooter's family?" Doc asked. "Could you get us in to see him?"

"His parents are summering on their yacht," Binka said. "But I can tell you where the house is. Maybe Scooter will want to talk."

"Good enough," Doc said, then turned to me. "I'm gonna shower. I've got whale in my hair. When I'm done, we're going to visit this kid and find out what he knows."

"We?" I repeated, surprised.

"Yeah. You're good at solving crimes. I want you along to help figure out what's going on here." Without even waiting for me to agree, Doc strode briskly around the corner to the outdoor shower.

"Why do you think Doc's so interested in solving this case?" I asked Summer.

She gave me a bemused look. "You really don't know?"

"No."

"Teddy, for a genius, sometimes you can be a real idiot."

"What's that supposed to mean?" I asked.

Before she could reply, Binka suddenly exclaimed, "Summer! I almost forgot! I called my PR person, and she wants to meet you ASAP. She's coming over for brunch tomorrow morning."

Summer groaned. "Binka! I told you I didn't want to talk to her."

"And I told you that was a mistake," Binka insisted. "Trish is great. You'll love her."

"But Teddy and I have to help Doc figure out who blew up the whale."

"Believe me, no one wants whoever did that to go to jail more than I do. I mean look at this." Binka pointed to her plate glass windows, which had random pieces of blubber and viscera stuck to them like barnacles. "I just had these cleaned! And now they are covered with whale glop! But this won't take too much time. It's only a little brunch."

"We're going to be really busy with this case," Summer told her. "Teddy and I were thinking that we should interview everyone who lives along the beach to see if they saw anything suspicious." She gave me an imploring look, which I realized meant she wanted me to back her up.

"That's right!" I said quickly. "And I was thinking, maybe we ought to talk to some of the surfers, too."

"Good idea!" Summer exclaimed. "Like that guy Sharky."

"Sharky?" Binka laughed. "What do you want to talk to that lunatic for?"

"You know Sharky?" Summer asked, obviously trying to distract Binka from the subject of brunch with Trish.

"Everyone in the Colony knows Sharky," Binka told her. "He surfs this beach all the time. But his brain is fried from spending so much time in the sun. He's always going on about some crazy thing or another. A few weeks ago, he said he'd seen Russian submarines patrolling the coast. And before that, he swore a megalodon had tried to eat him."

"He thinks that and he's still surfing?" I asked, stunned. A megalodon was a prehistoric shark the size of a humpback whale. They'd been extinct for eons, but still, if I thought I saw one, I wouldn't have gone back in the water.

Binka said, "If Sharky thought there were piranhas armed with machines guns out there, he'd still go surfing. I've seen him out during thunderstorms and sewage leaks. Why do you even want to talk to him?"

"If he's out here all the time, maybe he's noticed some unusual activity," Summer suggested.

"Although maybe he *isn't* the most reliable witness," I reminded her. "I mean, he thought someone had stolen part of the beach."

"The beach?" Binka echoed. "How could someone steal a beach?"

"I don't know," I said. "But Sharky claims someone made off with a couple tons of sand a few nights ago."

Binka gave a short, sharp burst of laughter. "The sand moves around all the time! Four weeks ago, the beach in front of my place eroded so badly that I had to have that stepladder taped to the stairs. But that's just nature! Some day, the tide will shift again and the sand will come back."

"Sharky believes a thief did this," Summer insisted.

"Well that's just crazy," Binka said. "Sharky's really lost it this time."

"I don't think so."

The last statement caught us by surprise. We all turned around to find the pool guy had returned to the deck. He was now armed with an industrial-strength skimmer to help him get the whale gunk out of the pool.

"What do you mean?" I asked him.

"I was surfing up at County Line a couple mornings ago," the pool guy replied. "And some folks were saying that a bunch of sand had been stolen from there, too. I figured they didn't know what they were talking about, but now . . . Well, I guess they were right. Someone really *is* stealing the beaches."

I looked from the pool guy to Binka to Summer, trying to get my mind around this new revelation. It instantly brought up two huge questions.

How could someone possibly steal so much sand? And why?

THE PATSY

As Binka had said, the Derman family had another house only twenty miles from the Colony. It had seemed ridiculous to me that a family would have two homes so close together. But it turned out that distance in LA was very different from where I lived, because of traffic.

In the Texas Hill Country, the only real traffic was all the tourists pulling into the FunJungle parking lot in the morning. If you wanted to go anywhere else, the roads were almost empty, so traveling twenty miles was no big deal. I knew people who regularly drove to Houston for dinner, and that was over two hundred miles away.

However, we were in bumper-to-bumper traffic all the way from Malibu to Bel Air. The thousands of people who had gone to the beach for the day were heading back into the city, and then there was rush-hour traffic as well. Three separate car wrecks snarled everything up even worse. Getting through it all took us nearly an hour and a half.

But once we reached Bel Air, things were different. Bel Air was a wealthy section of Los Angeles, located on the southern flank of the mountain range that cut through the city, right next to Beverly Hills. Not only was there no traffic; there didn't seem to be many people at all. While the homes in the Colony had been crammed together, the ones in Bel Air were spaced far apart on massive properties, most of which were surrounded by imposing walls or towering hedges. There were no sidewalks or bike lanes along the narrow, winding roads.

"Doesn't look like anyone walks around here," I noted.

"Maybe they're all exhausted by walking from their bedrooms to their kitchens," Doc suggested. "That looks to be at least a mile in some of these places."

Even though Doc was joking, it didn't seem to be that much of an exaggeration. The homes that we could see beyond the walls were enormous and sprawling.

Cass was driving us in her official NOAA vehicle, a pickup truck with an extended cab; Doc was in the passenger seat, while Summer and I sat in the back. The flensing knives and other autopsy tools were rattling around in the bed.

When Doc had invited her to come with us to question

Scooter, Cass had jumped at the chance. (Although, like the rest of us, she'd used Binka's outdoor shower to clean off first.) Cass seemed just as eager as Doc to find out what had really happened to the dead whale—and she also didn't want to spend any more time getting yelled at by wealthy homeowners in the Colony. For most of our drive, she had been on the phone with the Coast Guard, trying to arrange for the remains of the whale to be towed out to sea; as far as she was concerned, there was no way to determine the cause of death with what was left.

Between calls, we had managed to learn a little bit more about Cass. She had grown up poor, in an area of Los Angeles called Compton, but done well in school and earned a scholarship to the University of California at Santa Cruz. Even though Compton wasn't much farther from the beach than Bel Air, Cass still hadn't been able to go often; she was ten before she had ever even seen the ocean. But UC Santa Cruz was located only a short walk from Monterey Bay. On the first day, Cass had seen a whale from campus and instantly fallen in love. The beasts were staggeringly large and yet surprisingly graceful. She wanted to know everything about them.

She also knew a lot about the history of Los Angeles. "A lot of these properties used to have normal-size homes," she explained, weaving through the serpentine roads of Bel Air. "But now, only the exceptionally rich can afford to buy here. So they just scrape the old places off and build these monstrosities with more rooms than anyone knows what to do with."

As she said this, we rounded a curve and came upon a mansion so colossal that it made all the others look tiny in comparison.

The entire summit of a small mountain had been removed, creating a mesa upon which a modern-day castle had been erected.

"Here we are," Cass said.

"This is Scooter's house?" I asked, surprised.

"Well, it's his parents," Cass replied. "This is the address Binka gave us."

A large gate blocked the entrance to the property, and next to that was a guardhouse the size of my home. The two security men stationed there were both dressed like secret service agents, with dark suits, sunglasses, and earpieces. One stepped outside as we pulled up and eyed us suspiciously.

"State your business here," he demanded gruffly.

"We're here to talk to Scooter," Cass said.

"And you would be . . . ?"

"People he'll want to see." Cass flashed a disarming smile. "Tell him that we're here from the National Oceanic and Atmospheric Administration. We've talked to Chase, and we know Scooter was framed for blowing up the whale. But we want to hear his side of the story. Especially the part about Sadie."

The security man considered this for a moment, then returned to the guardhouse and made a call. A minute later, he stepped back outside, not looking nearly as gruff anymore. "Scooter would like to talk. Follow this road up to the main house and he'll meet you there." He glanced into the bed of the truck, then said, "For safety reasons, I'll have to ask you to leave the weapons here."

There didn't seem to be much point in arguing that the autopsy tools weren't really weapons. So we allowed the security men to remove them. The gates swung open, revealing a two-lane stone driveway that snaked up the mountainside. We headed along it.

Even though we'd had a glimpse of the mansion from the road, it was even more staggering up close. It appeared to be larger than my entire middle school, with an enormous four-story central building and two-story wings that extended out on both sides. The driveway led to a circular parking area big enough for thirty cars, with a giant fountain in the middle that seemed as if it had been stolen from Versailles. Another branch of the driveway dipped underground, indicating that there was another parking area below us.

A butler in a three-piece suit was waiting by the front door to greet us, but before he could, Scooter emerged from the house. He had showered and changed since we had last seen him, although his new clothes looked almost exactly the same as his old ones. He looked nervous and jittery. "Hey!" he said, running over to greet us as we climbed out of the truck. "I'm Scooter."

"We know," Doc said. "We came here to see you."

"Oh yeah. Right." Scooter nodded. "You're the guys from the beach, right? The ones who chased us? Back there, I thought you wanted to arrest us."

"We want to know what happened," Cass told him. "We talked to Chase, and he told us a bit about how you were framed, but he couldn't remember everything. . . ."

"Makes sense. Chase was pretty wasted last night." Scooter laughed, thinking back to it. "He puked like ten times after we left that party."

"So we were hoping you could fill in the blanks," Cass concluded.

We had all discussed the story we should tell Scooter on the drive. Cass felt that we could get away with lying to him, because we weren't actually law enforcement, and not subject to the same laws that the police were. The story had obviously worked. Scooter was so eager to talk to us, it never even occurred to him to ask what Summer and I were doing there. He just led us into his house while rattling off his hazy recollections of the previous night.

"The party was at our friend Darla's house," he said. "She's in the Colony too, so of course the whale was all anyone was talking about. It was right out there for everyone to see, being all gross and smelly and stuff. Darla's place was pretty far down the beach, but we could still see the whale from there, you know, because it was big."

The entry foyer of the house was large enough to play tennis in, a great expanse of marble floor flanked by sweeping grand staircases. Scooter led us past them, into an honest-to-goodness ballroom. It was completely empty, save for two massive crystal chandeliers.

"How did you meet this Sadie?" Cass prodded, her voice echoing in the empty room.

Scooter said, "She was out on the deck, by the pool, talking to some other girls, and she was really pretty, so Chase wanted to talk to her and asked me to be his wingman. It was *her* idea to blow up the whale, not ours."

"How did it come up?" I asked.

"I can't remember exactly. We'd been talking to her for a while. Me and Chase and her had gone out onto the beach to try to see the whale better, and I think Sadie just said that it'd be a great prank if someone blew it up." Scooter led us out of the ballroom into another expansive space that appeared to be for hosting parties. There were multiple sitting areas and two separate bars, although the most notable thing about it was the view. The entire rear wall was glass, looking out onto an Olympic-sized swimming pool lined by chaise lounges. Beyond that was a stunning panorama of Los Angeles that stretched from downtown all the way to the beach.

"And what did you say to that?" Doc asked Scooter.

"We agreed. Although we didn't realize Sadie was going to blow up the whale so badly. She *tricked* us into doing that. We thought it'd be only a little explosion."

"A *little* explosion?" Cass repeated.

"Yeah. Sadie said the whale would just pop, like a balloon. Not go off like a volcano. She had the whole thing figured out. She even had the dynamite and the detonators."

"She just happened to have dynamite?" I asked.

"Yeah. In her car. She said her father worked in construction, so it was no big deal. She could get that stuff any time she wanted to."

Summer gaped at him, stunned. "And none of this seemed suspicious to you at the time?"

"Well . . . no," Scooter replied. "But then, we were pretty drunk."

The back doors to the house were open onto the yard. Scooter led us outside. In addition to the pool, there was an outdoor kitchen, a formal garden with more fountains, a tennis court, a basketball court, a beach volleyball court, a bocce pit, and a lawn flanked by rows of cypress trees.

We followed Scooter to a cabana by the pool. Inside it were several couches, a bar, and a flat-screen TV. "Any of you want anything to drink?" Scooter asked.

The adults asked for water, while Summer and I requested sodas. Scooter got them all out of the fridge, then uncapped a beer for himself.

The sun was starting to set, and the clouds over the Pacific were glowing red and orange. The lights of Los Angeles sparkled in the twilight. In other circumstances, it would have been a pleasure to just sit there and take in the view.

"So let me get this straight," Cass said. "You and Chase met a random woman at a party. She suggested that you put dynamite into the corpse of a dead whale as a joke . . . and you went along with it?"

"We thought it would be funny!" Scooter explained, like we were somehow missing the point. "All those tourists would be gathered around, and suddenly, the whale would go bang! Like a balloon popping. Maybe it'd scare some people, but that would be it. We didn't know Sadie was going to put way more explosive inside than she told us— and that whale guts were going to fly all over the place and ruin people's houses. She tricked us!"

"You really go to Harvard?" I asked, incredulous.

"That's right," Scooter said.

Summer asked, "How much did your parents have to donate to the school for you to get in?"

"Only a library," Scooter replied.

"Who put the dynamite in the whale?" Cass inquired. "You and Chase?"

Scooter shook his head. "No. Sadie said she'd take care of everything. Except setting it off. She said we ought to handle that. So she gave us the detonator today, right before the explosion."

Doc stiffened in surprise. "Sadie was there today? When you did this?"

"Of course."

"Where was she?"

Scooter started to answer, then frowned. "I don't know. She said she'd be nearby, because she wanted to watch the whale blow up. But I didn't see her afterward. Of course, I didn't get much of a chance to look around, because you all chased me away."

"You fled the scene," Cass corrected. "There's a difference."

"The point is, Sadie was there beforehand."

Cass asked, "Did you get her last name, by any chance?"

"Er . . . no. She never said it. And, to be honest, I'm not totally sure her name was Sadie. I *think* that was it, but Chase thought she might have said Zadie."

"Or maybe she made up a fake name," Summer suggested.

Scooter gaped at her in surprise. "I never thought of that! Yeah, I guess she could have."

"Can you describe Sadie?" said Doc.

"Yeah. She was *really* pretty."

"So you've said," Cass noted. "Can you give us any more detail? What color were her eyes? Or her hair?"

Scooter considered that, then frowned again. "I'm not sure. It was pretty dark last night when I met her."

"What about today, on the beach?" I asked. "It wasn't dark then."

"No, but she was wearing a big, floppy hat. And sunglasses. And her hair was pulled back. I think it was dark, though. Black or brown. Although, now that I think about it, maybe it was blond."

Doc sighed with exasperation. "You talked to this woman all night, met her again this morning, and you don't even know what color her hair is?"

"I'm not like a big detail guy, okay?"

"Any idea how old she was?" Summer questioned.

"Somewhere between twenty and thirty. Although I guess she could have been older with a lot of plastic surgery."

"That describes half the women in Malibu," Cass grumbled.

"Did you even *look* at this woman while you were talking to her?" Summer asked.

"Like I said, it was dark!" Scooter protested. "And today I was more focused on getting the detonator."

I asked him, "Is there anything you can tell us about Sadie at all?"

Scooter furrowed his brow in concentration, then suddenly lit up. "Oh! She had a weird laugh!"

"How so?" Cass asked.

"It was really squeaky, like this." Scooter imitated it, making three short, high-pitched chirps. It was definitely weird. It sounded like a cartoon mouse with the hiccups.

I looked to the others. "Well, that's something."

"Sure," Summer said. "Now all we have to do is go tickle every woman in Los Angeles and see what her laugh sounds like."

I looked out at the enormous city sprawled below us, thinking about how many millions of people lived there. Finding just one of them was daunting.

"Assuming this woman is even still in Los Angeles at all," Cass said. "It's possible that she left the city. Or even the country. Locating her again without a decent description— or even a name—is going to be almost impossible."

"But you believe me, right?" Scooter looked to us hopefully. "You believe that this wasn't my idea?"

"Yes," Doc said. "It's obvious that you're not the kind of person who has any ideas at all."

"Thanks!" Scooter said, not realizing that he'd been insulted. "So, do you think you can prove that I'm innocent? Are you taking my case?"

"We're not detectives," Cass told him.

"You're not?" Scooter asked, surprised.

"No," Cass said. "Didn't your security man tell you that we were from NOAA?"

"They did. But I didn't know what that meant. I figured NOAA was like the FBI, but for whale-related crimes or something."

"It's the National Oceanic and Atmospheric Administration," Cass explained.

"Oh. Well, you still came to hear my side of the story. So that means you want to figure out what really happened. Which is more than I can say for the police." There was now desperation in Scooter's eyes. "They already came here today, wanting to arrest me. The security guys told them I wasn't here, and the police didn't challenge it, because they know who my father is. They can't just bust in and arrest me. But Dad says they're probably going to get a warrant soon, so . . . until then, I need to get out of town."

I was suddenly aware of a whirring noise in the distance. A helicopter was approaching the mansion.

"Where are you going?" Summer asked Scooter.

"I don't know," he admitted. "Dad arranged this. He thought it'd be best if he kept it all a secret."

The butler emerged from the mansion, wheeling two large suitcases across the patio. "You're all packed," he told Scooter.

Scooter accepted the luggage, then looked back to us. "I'll pay you to clear my name."

"How much?" I asked.

Although, at the exact same time, Summer said, "We don't need your money."

"Speak for yourself," I told her. "I'm poor, and my house just burned down."

The helicopter was now so close, it was hard to hear over the noise it made. There was no official helipad on the property; the lawn was almost wide enough to handle it—but not quite. As the copter came down, its rotors nicked the tips off several cypress trees and created a gale-force wind that blew all the cushions off the chaise lounges and into the pool.

"I'll pay whatever it costs!" Scooter shouted over the noise. "Find Sadie! She's the real criminal here, not me!"

With that, he hurried across the lawn and clambered into the waiting helicopter with his luggage. The moment he had closed the door behind him, the aircraft lifted up and whisked him away toward the city.

"It's just not fair," Cass said, watching the helicopter disappear among the million lights of Los Angeles. "If some kid from South Central was suspected of vandalizing Malibu like that, the police would have knocked down his door and hauled him to jail. Meanwhile, that moron gets to flee the country because his parents are filthy rich."

"The police still have his friend Chase, though," Summer pointed out. She looked a bit unsettled by Cass's comment; after all, Summer was filthy rich herself.

"Not for long, though," Cass presumed. "I'm sure Chase's family will spring him too, if they haven't already. And then he'll probably be on a private helicopter out of the country as well." She booted another of the cushions into the pool. "Point being, these privileged jerks get to glide through life, never being held accountable for anything. This Sadie—or whatever her name was—knew exactly what she was doing when she went looking for suckers to help her out. No poor kid from LA would agree to blow up a whale as a prank. They'd know that if anything went wrong, they'd go to jail and their lives would be ruined. But Scooter and Chase didn't give it a second thought. Even now, that dimwit doesn't seem to have any idea what's really going on here."

"Um . . . neither do I," I admitted.

"I'll explain it over dinner," Cass told me. "I'm starving."

THE SUSPECTS

Beverly Hills was just south of Bel Air. Cass drove us through it, pointing out all the fancy restaurants where she claimed the rich and famous ate and dinner could cost what most people made in a week. But according to her, none of them served the best meal in the city.

For that, we went to a gas station.

A taco truck was parked only twenty feet away from the pumps. Despite the unusual location, it obviously wasn't a secret; twenty people were waiting in line. We got carnitas tacos, horchata, chips, and guacamole, then went to a park across the street and sat at a picnic table to eat.

The whole meal cost us less than forty dollars—and it was incredible.

"This explosion wasn't the work of pranksters," Cass

declared, digging into her tacos. "Before I met back up with you in Malibu, I called a friend in the bomb unit for the army. She said the amount of explosive you'd need to blow up a whale of that size isn't the kind of thing that normal people could get their hands on."

"Not even from a construction site?" Summer asked.

Cass shook her head. "Not even there. And construction sites aren't about to leave explosives lying around anyhow. That story Sadie fed Chase and Scooter is a bunch of malarkey. Whoever did this was a pro, and this Sadie set the guys up to take the fall. I didn't think to get a photo of the detonator, but my friend is betting that was a dummy as well. The real bomber probably triggered the blast from a lot farther away."

"Then we ought to tell the police about this," I said.

"I *tried.*" Cass plunked a chip into her guacamole. "Back on the beach today. But thanks to us, they have Chase Buckingham fleeing the scene with a detonator. He's definitely guilty of *something*—and his father has been a thorn in the side of the sheriff's department for years, filing all sorts of suits against them. So law enforcement is thrilled to have this kid go down in flames. Social media's having a field day with the story."

I knew about that. Summer had shown me during the drive to dinner. The story of the exploding whale was trending everywhere—and the idea that some privileged rich kid had been arrested for the crime was too good to ignore. Public opinion had already convicted Chase. If the kid hadn't been such a jerk to us, I might have felt bad for him.

"So the police aren't going to be any help," Summer concluded. "If we want to know who blew up that whale, we're on our own."

Cass and Doc both nodded.

"Now, the reason for the explosion is pretty evident," Doc said. "Someone didn't want Cass to perform that autopsy. Which indicates she would have discovered evidence that the death was suspicious."

"You mean the whale was murdered?" I asked.

"Possibly." Cass polished off her first taco. "But more likely, the whale died as the result of some human behavior, and whoever was responsible wanted to cover it up."

"What kind of behavior?" Summer asked. "How could someone kill a whale?"

"Oh, there are all sorts of ways," Cass said. "First of all, there's actual whaling, where someone hunts down the animals and kills them on purpose. They harpoon the animal, then flense it with the same tools I was going to use for the autopsy. There are still a few countries that do it. It's illegal in US waters, but that doesn't mean someone wouldn't do it here anyhow. Thanks to our policies, we have relatively healthy whale populations. That's not the case everywhere else. So maybe someone came looking to poach some of our whales."

I took a sip of horchata. "But if someone had harpooned that whale, you would have noticed even before the autopsy, right? It would have been obvious."

"Not necessarily," Cass replied. "If the wound was on the side of the whale that was lying on the beach, we wouldn't have seen it. It's possible that someone attempted to kill it, but things didn't go well and it escaped, only to die later. Or maybe some awful person was just trying to maim it for no good reason."

"Like the sea lion that Doc came out here to look at," Summer said, heaping a chip with guacamole. "The one that got shot in the face."

"Yes," Doc agreed, "although, admittedly, I think this is the least likely scenario. If someone was actively whaling, that would require a large ship specially designed for the act, which would be hard to move through these waters without being noticed by the Coast Guard. . . ."

"But not impossible," Cass said. "There are thousands of square miles of marine habitat off California and less than fifteen Coast Guard vessels to patrol it all. And it'd be even easier for someone looking to simply harm a whale to get away with it. All they'd need would be a fast enough boat and a big enough weapon."

Doc looked like he didn't fully believe that, but for some reason, he didn't argue the point. Instead, he said, "I think a ship strike is much more likely."

"Ship strike?" I repeated.

"That's when a ship hits a whale by accident," Cass explained. "Like an oil tanker or a cargo vessel. Fully loaded cargo ships can weigh over two hundred thousand tons and travel at nearly thirty miles an hour. So they can do serious damage, even to an animal the size of a blue whale."

"How often does that happen?" I asked.

"Sadly, we don't know." Cass dug into her second taco. "These ships are so big, they often have no idea that they've even hit a whale at all."

"Like the one in San Francisco this summer!" Summer exclaimed.

"What are you talking about?" I asked blankly.

"Oh," Summer said, as understanding dawned on her. "It was when you'd gone camping."

That would have been in mid-July. After spending a few days with Summer's family outside Yellowstone National Park—during which I had solved another crime—my parents and I had gone into the backcountry for five days. We had hiked south of Yellowstone Lake to an area that was the farthest point from a road—or any other civilization—in the lower forty-eight states. There had been no cell service there, and we had been fully off the grid the entire time.

"This big cargo ship came into San Francisco Bay," Summer explained. "And there was a dead whale smashed right on the front of it."

"A fin whale," Cass added. "One of the biggest types of whales there are, and the crew hadn't even noticed. That's how big these ships are."

"It hit the whale and just kept going?" I asked, horrified.

"Yeah. It was awful," Summer said. "I'll show you a photo." She dug out her phone and started searching.

"That's okay," I told her. "I've seen enough dead whale lately."

Cass said, "The shipping lanes around here are designed to try to prevent ship strikes, but they still happen. You can tell the ships to avoid where the whales are most likely to be, but you can't tell the whales to avoid the ships. Plus, whales aren't very nimble. They're too big. A dolphin can dart out of a ship's path at the last instant. A whale can't."

"Toxins are another possibility," Doc said, scraping up the last of the guacamole with a tortilla chip.

"Right," Cass agreed. "The amount of poison humans dump in the oceans is insane. There's oil spills, runoff from storm drains, illegal dumping of chemicals. We're slowly poisoning every sea creature on the planet. A really bad chemical dump can wipe out everything for miles—even something as big as a whale."

Summer made a face of disgust.

Doc finished off a taco. "There are other types of deadly pollution, namely plastics."

"Oh," I said. "I know about that. Like the Great Pacific Garbage Patch."

"What's that?" Summer asked.

"It's a collection of floating garbage that's the size of Texas," I responded.

Summer gasped. "Really? That's terrible."

"It is," Cass said. "And that's only the tip of the iceberg, so to speak. Right now, about eight million tons of plastic escapes into the ocean every year. That's the equivalent of setting five garbage bags full of trash on every single foot of coastline around the world. And if we don't make changes soon, things are only going to get worse. Plastic production is growing at an astronomical pace. In 1950, less than two and a half million tons were produced worldwide. In 2015, that was four hundred forty-eight million tons. And production will double by 2050. By some estimates, within a decade or so, there will be more pounds of plastic in the oceans than pounds of fish."

I gulped at the thought of that, then considered the

picnic table in front of me. Our tacos had all come in plastic clamshell containers, and even though we had passed on taking straws, our drink cups were plastic as well. I looked back at the taco truck line across the street. There were now thirty people in it, and each of them was probably ordering for several people, all of whom would also get their food in plastic containers. Which meant that a single business might use a few thousand disposable plastic objects every night, all of which would probably end up in the trash. "Looks like we're part of the problem," I observed.

"*Everyone* is part of the problem," Cass said with a sigh. "Plastic is inescapable. It's everywhere."

"And it can kill a whale?" Summer asked.

"Absolutely," Cass said. "For example, we've found sperm whales with stomachs full of plastic. They gulp it down by accident while eating their prey, and since it's hard to digest, it can accumulate over the years. If a whale's belly is full of garbage, it can't eat as much as it needs to, which affects its overall health. Whales need to consume fresh water to survive, just like us, and they get most of that from the fish they eat. If they don't get enough fish, they don't get enough water. So we actually have cases of whales dying from dehydration due to plastic ingestion."

Summer whistled in surprise, then considered her garbage. "We should probably recycle this."

"Good luck with that," Cass grumbled. "The recycling bins in this park only take glass and paper, and even if you took that plastic home and put it in the recycling bin, the chances are very slim that it would really get recycled. And that's in California, which has a strong recycling program. Plenty of states—and an awful lot of countries—don't."

I nodded understanding. "Okay, plastic is bad for whales. But if the one on the beach died from eating a bunch of it, that's on all of humanity, right? Why would someone want to cover that up?"

Cass shrugged. "Could be someone from the plastics industry who just doesn't want the bad publicity. Or maybe a container full of plastic bags fell off a cargo ship and dumped a couple million in the ocean. More than five hundred containers go overboard each year."

"Both of those sound kind of far-fetched," Doc said, although not as gruffly as I would have normally suspected.

"I suppose," Cass admitted. "I'm just spitballing here. If you have any brilliant ideas, I'd love to hear them."

Doc considered that, then seemed upset that he didn't have anything else to contribute.

"Maybe it's tied into the theft of all the sand," I suggested.

Doc turned to me, surprised. "Don't tell me you took that lunatic surfer seriously. . . ."

"Sharky was right!" Summer exclaimed. "Binka's pool guy said the same thing happened at a place called County Line."

Cass swallowed the last of her tacos, looking concerned. "This is real?"

"I guess," I said. "Maybe, if someone was using some kind of big machine to steal the sand, it hurt the whale in some way."

"What kind of big machine would this be?" Doc asked, sounding far more brusque with me than he had with Cass.

"I don't know," I confessed. "But if someone's stealing tons of sand at once, they're probably not doing it with a pail and a shovel."

"I'll make some calls," Cass said. "Maybe someone else at NOAA's heard about this happening somewhere else. Or knows what it might be about." She wiped the grease off her hands on a balled-up napkin. "Which brings us to the final point. Everything we've mentioned here—ship strikes, pollution, dumping toxic waste, stealing beaches— it's all large-scale stuff. A fisherman didn't accidentally kill this whale with a thirty-foot motorboat and then hire a professional demolition expert to get rid of the evidence. Whoever was behind this has very deep pockets."

"You mean, like a corporation," Summer said.

"Right," Cass agreed. "I think that's what we're up against here. We just have to figure out which one."

I felt myself shivering. In part, this was because I was cold. Unlike Texas, Los Angeles wasn't humid in the summer; now that the sun had gone down, it was much chillier than I had expected. But I was also concerned. From experience, I knew that going up against a corrupt corporation could be very dangerous.

We had all finished our dinner, creating a disturbing amount of plastic garbage.

"I guess we really ought to at least *try* to recycle this, rather than just tossing it," Cass said. "I'll take it home to put in my bin and hope for the best." She stood and began to gather everything.

Doc snapped to his feet. "Let me help you with that," he said, and collected all the trash with her.

"What a gentleman," Cass said teasingly, then led the way back to the truck. Doc stayed by her side, leaving Summer and me to follow.

As I watched the two of them together, I suddenly had a moment of understanding. "The reason Doc wants to help with this case . . . It's because he likes Cass, right?"

Summer gave me an amused look. "Took you long enough to figure that out."

"When did *you* know he liked her?"

"From pretty much the first moment we met her. You didn't see the way he was looking at her?"

"Uh, no. I was kind of focused on the giant dead whale on the beach."

"There were like a million other signs as well. Starting with the fact that he agreed to come out here to deal with the blind sea lion instead of pawning it off on someone else. Obviously, he was just looking for an excuse to see her. He certainly knew the dead whale was on that beach; it's been there for three days. So he probably called Cass and said he'd be in Malibu and would love a chance to observe the autopsy. Because nothing's as romantic as dissecting a thirty-ton corpse. Men will do anything to get close to a woman they like."

"That's not true," I said.

"Within five minutes of meeting me, you agreed to go swimming in the hippo pool at FunJungle."

"That was for a case!"

"Yeah. I'm sure it had nothing to do with the fact that you thought I was pretty." Summer fluttered her eyelashes at me.

"Don't forget, the whole thing was your idea. I guess maybe you were interested in *me*, too." I fake fluttered my eyelashes right back at her.

"Maybe a little," Summer said with a smile. "But back to Doc. His plans to cozy up to Cass during the autopsy went sideways when the whale blew up. So he came up with a whole new scheme: help figure out who did it."

"But why ask for our help? Don't you think he'd rather be with Cass alone?"

"Two reasons." Summer ticked them off on her fingers. "One: Doc actually wants to solve this crime. Because that will make him look good to Cass. And you've shown you're good at that. Two: he's probably nervous around her, so having us here helps."

"Doc's nervous? No way. Mom says that when he's in surgery, he never even breaks a sweat."

"This is different. As far as I know, Doc hasn't seen anyone since his divorce, and that was like five years ago. Which means it could be at least two decades since he last went on a date. The guy has even less game than you."

"Hey!"

Summer grinned to let me know she was joking. "All I'm saying is, don't be surprised if Doc wants us close by until all this is over."

"But what if it gets dangerous?"

Summer laughed. "Teddy, when you're involved, the question is never 'What if it gets dangerous?' The question is 'When?'"

I sighed, hoping that this time, that wouldn't be true.

But as usual, Summer was right.

GARBAGE

I called my parents on the way back to the Colony.
I wanted to catch my father before he left for Argentina the next day. It was getting late in Texas, but they had stayed up to talk to me. They were both spending the night in Mom's office. It was cramped, but since they could hear the chimpanzees in the exhibit next door, they said it reminded them of Africa.

Of course, they immediately suspected that I had been near the whale when it exploded. They had seen it on the news and knew it was right down the beach from where I was staying. I admitted that I had been close enough to get slimed, but omitted my investigating the crime. Since I had ended up in danger on previous cases, I knew they wouldn't want me involved. Telling them that Doc was there to keep an eye on me wouldn't have done any good; instead, I feared they would be upset at him for asking for my help. I felt bad about not being entirely truthful with them, but I didn't want to have an argument over the phone while in the truck with Doc, Cass, and Summer. Besides, I was doing my best to stay safe; with the exception of the exploding whale, I hadn't been in any danger at all so far.

By the time Cass dropped us all back at Binka's house, I was exhausted. I was still on Texas time, and it had been a long day. Summer felt the same way. Kandace and Binka were nestled on the sofa with glasses of wine, catching up. They invited us to join them, but I just wanted to go to bed. Doc was staying in a small, private house on the property that Binka referred to as a casita. Summer and I each had our own guest room. Binka had so many, she wasn't even sure of the exact number herself. Mine had a private bathroom and balcony overlooking the ocean. I went right to bed and was asleep within seconds of lying down.

I woke just after dawn.

Even though it was early, I was well rested enough to know I wouldn't fall back asleep again, and the roar of the surf outside was beckoning.

I padded downstairs in my bare feet. The wineglasses were still on the coffee table, next to an empty bottle. There was a note from Binka saying *Summer and Teddy—We sleep late around here. If you get up early, feel free to eat anything you want.* I made myself a bagel with cream cheese and cut up some fresh plums; they were delicious.

Then I went out the sliding glass door to the deck and made my way to the sand. As I shifted from the wooden stairs to the ladder that had been taped to them, I noticed that the sand had shifted slightly during the night. The day before, the ladder's legs had rested on the beach. Today, they were buried two inches below a new layer of wet sand the ocean had brought in, although the ground was still significantly lower at Binka's than at any of her neighbors'.

Most coastal beaches in the United States run north–south, but Malibu is unusual in that it goes east–west. So the sun was rising at the far end of the beach, where the lagoon was. I headed that way.

The dead whale was gone.

Well, most of it was.

The night before, while we had been eating tacos in Beverly Hills, the Coast Guard had removed the large pieces of the carcass that remained after the explosion. Cass said they had simply dragged it all out to sea and let it sink to the bottom, where it would provide food for thousands of marine animals. This was what happened to most dead whales; it was known to scientists as a "whale fall." My father had shown me time-lapse videos of it happening;

over the course of a few weeks, an entire whale would be reduced to bones by crabs, lobsters, hagfish, shrimp, snails, and sleeper sharks, and then even the bones themselves would be consumed by invertebrates like zombie worms. So there was no point in letting a good carcass go to waste.

Of course, the Coast Guard hadn't been able to remove every last remnant of the carcass. There were still plenty of whale bits strewn far and wide by the explosion: strips of blubbery skin littered the beach; gooey lumps of viscera lay on rooftops; pieces of lung and heart and stomach were splattered on walls, decks, and windows. (The night before, Binka had reported that many of the owners hadn't been able to hire cleaning crews right away, as there was a short supply of people who were able—or willing—to clean up all the gunk.) The worst of it was a six-foot-long strip of intestine which had somehow survived the blast intact; it stretched across the beach by Jackson Cross's seawall, not far from where the bottom of the staircase from his pool deck hung a foot above the sand. It looked like an enormous, bloated earthworm, and it reeked like rotten seafood. There was still so much whale around that even the hundreds of seagulls that had winged in for the feast hadn't been able to consume it all. Most were sitting on the beach, their bellies swollen, looking as though they had gorged themselves until they could no longer fly.

What was *really* shocking, though, was the amount of garbage on the beach.

The day before, I had been far too distracted by the giant carcass to pay much attention to anything else. But now, as I walked along the waterline, trying to avoid stepping on fragments of bone or pads of decaying blubber, I noticed that there was plenty of man-made junk on the sand as well. Almost all of it was plastic: a broken pink toy bucket and shovel that had either been abandoned or forgotten, grocery bags tangled up among strands of seaweed, candy wrappers, collapsed water bottles, bottle caps, fast-food containers, straws, and dozens of cigarette filters. I picked up the bucket and started collecting the trash I found.

There was a trench through the sand where the whale had lain, a furrow that had been gouged by the enormous head as it was dragged away. The tide had risen and fallen during the night, partly filling it with wet sand, but it was still deep enough that I had to step into it and climb back out the other side.

As I did, I noticed yet another piece of garbage, jutting from the sand at the very bottom of the trench: a piece of white paper. I tugged on it, expecting it to come up easily, but then found there was more of it than I had realized, buried so deeply that I had to get down on my knees and dig it up. It turned out to be most of a crushed beverage cup from a fast-food restaurant. *The Spot* was written on it in large red letters, followed by *famous burgers, fries, and shakes* in slightly smaller letters, and then, down at the bottom, it said *Carp*, which was possibly just a word fragment; the paper after the *p* had been torn away.

The cup was made the same way as pretty much all fast-food beverage cups, including the ones at FunJungle: mostly paper, but lined with plastic inside to give it some rigidity. It seemed relatively new. I plunked it into the bucket, then considered the trench. So far, I had only been concerned about garbage sitting on the beach. Now I wondered how much was buried under the sand.

"Looks like you and I had the same idea."

I turned, surprised, to find Jackson Cross standing at the edge of the trench. He was dressed for beachcombing, with a hooded sweatshirt, board shorts, and bare feet. He clutched a large plastic trash bag in his hand.

"You're picking up garbage too?" I asked.

"Every day." Jackson sighed heavily. "You'd think this stretch would be pretty free of garbage, because most everyone who comes out here could schlep their trash back into their homes, but they don't. Of course, even if they did, trash floats." He pointed to the pink bucket I was holding. "For all we know, someone could have left that on a beach in Japan or Australia and it floated all the way here." He held his bag open. "Want me to take that off your hands?"

"Thanks." The bucket was awfully full. I happily dropped it in the bag.

"Which way are you heading?" Jackson asked me.

I pointed in the direction of the lagoon. "I never got down there yesterday. Because of the whale."

"That's the way I'm heading too. Mind if I join you?"

"Sure," I said, thinking that Summer would freak out if she knew Jackson Cross was inviting me to walk with him. Given how famous he was, he seemed like a perfectly normal person.

We headed down the beach. A dog suddenly started barking.

I looked back to Jackson's home. A big, muscle-bound Rottweiler was at the railing of the pool deck. A private security man stood next to it; he looked like the human version of the dog, equally thickset and muscular.

"Shh, Tinkerbell!" Jackson said to the dog. "I'll be back soon!"

The dog kept barking, though.

"Gabriel, can you take her inside before she wakes the neighbors?" Jackson asked.

"Sure thing, Mr. Cross," the big man replied, then hustled the Rottweiler toward the house.

"Usually, I'd bring Tink along on these walks," Jackson told me. "But she's an eating machine and there's still whale everywhere. Yesterday, she ate goodness knows how much off the deck before I could find a safe place to put her. I couldn't exactly lock her in the house, since all my windows had shattered." He sounded understandably upset about everything that had happened.

"Sorry about your house," I said.

"I don't know who to be angrier at. Those hooligans Chase and Scooter or that woman from NOAA."

I looked up from collecting some cigarette butts, surprised. "Cass? She didn't blow up the whale."

"No, but she took her sweet time getting it off the beach. If it had been hauled away on day one, like all of us had requested, then Chase and Scooter wouldn't have had the chance to blow it up."

"Oh." I had to admit that was a good point. If it was my house that had been drenched in guts from a whale I'd asked to have removed, I'd probably be angry too. "Do you know Chase and Scooter?"

"Well enough to know they'd both think something like this would be funny." Jackson picked up a wayward plastic fork and dropped it in the trash bag. "I know their parents better. Scooter's are lovely. They've already emailed everyone in the Colony, apologizing for what their son did and offering to pay for our repairs. The Buckinghams, on the other hand . . . Let's just say they don't have many fans here."

"Why's that?"

"Chase's father is a lawyer who got very successful filing frivolous lawsuits. And any time he has an issue with anyone, no matter how small, he threatens legal action." He pointed to a few of the houses we were passing. "He sued Jasper Wingate over some business venture they went into together that flopped. He sued Hrishi Argawal for slander. He sued Wes and Nancy Smith for building an addition to their house that blocked his view. Even though he lives five houses away from them! The addition wasn't affecting him at all, and still he won, and they had to tear part of their house down. That's it right there."

We were passing a large, modern home with a similar design to Binka's. The Smiths' house was the one we had caught up to Chase in front of. I remembered Nancy. She was the bleached-blond woman who had talked to Skip Howell as he'd been taking Chase into custody the day before. She had told Skip about all the damage the exploded whale had done to her deck. It occurred to me that if someone was really angry at Chase Buckingham's father, then maybe framing Chase for a crime would be a good way to get revenge.

As for Scooter, it was possible that, as Chase's friend, he'd just gotten caught up in the plot. Maybe Sadie or Zadie or whatever her name was had only been hired to trick Chase into being the patsy, but Scooter had gamely gone along with it.

I considered the Smiths' mansion as we passed. The area where they'd had to remove the addition was still under construction. Despite the loss, the house was still massive. "That's a nice home," I observed. "What business are they in?"

"No one knows for sure," Jackson replied, then lowered his voice to a whisper. "Although the rumor is Wes made all his money in arms dealing."

I figured that someone who sold weapons could easily get their hands on dynamite. Or perhaps dynamite hadn't been used to blow up the whale at all. Chase and Scooter said Sadie had *told* them she would get dynamite. Maybe some sort of military explosives had been used instead. That would certainly explain the size of the blast.

But as intrigued as I was by this angle, there was another question I had to ask Jackson Cross. "Did Chase's father ever sue *you*?"

"Oh yes. Twice."

"Twice?"

"Both ridiculous. The first time, he said Tinkerbell destroyed some expensive imported plants in his yard. Even though there was blatant evidence that coyotes were responsible. He still made me go to court for it, though—and lost. And then, he had the gall to claim that one of his big plate windows had cracked because a DJ I hired for a party was too loud. That one got tossed out of court. Not a single home between mine and his had any damage at all. And now, look what his idiot son has done to *my* windows." Jackson gave a snort of disgust.

I found myself wondering if the Buckingham family might have blown up the whale to get even with Jackson somehow. Maybe they really thought he'd cracked their window and were trying to even the score. Or maybe Chase's father was annoyed that his lawsuits against Jackson had failed. In which case, there might not be a Sadie at all. She was a fiction Chase and Scooter had cooked up to pin the blame on. Which would explain why Scooter couldn't describe her worth a darn.

A big, soggy plastic bag marked *Malibu Chicken Shack* lay on the beach ahead of me. I picked it up, only to find it full of plastic clamshell to-go containers and tiny packets of ketchup and mayonnaise. It was at least two pounds of trash in one shot.

Jackson held out his trash bag for me to drop it in. "The closer we get to the public beach, the more garbage there is. The city has a lot of trash cans there, but it's stunning how many people don't use them. They get takeout, have a picnic, and then just leave everything right on the sand. I'd bet most of the cups and forks and stuff I find at my place washed up from there."

As I dropped my trash in his bag, another question

occurred to me. "Are there any other people in the Colony who might have a problem with you?"

Jackson arched an eyebrow at me in surprise. "Why?"

"I was just thinking your house got the worst of the explosion. Maybe someone *wanted* that to happen."

"Someone besides Chase and Scooter?"

"They said they were tricked into blowing the whale up by a woman named Sadie. Or Zadie. They couldn't remember."

"I don't know any woman with either of those names."

"It probably wasn't her real one."

Jackson considered me as we walked. "You're a real junior sleuth, aren't you? To be honest, when you're famous, there's all sorts of people who have it in for you. Hundreds, if not thousands, of people you've never even met before."

"How's that?"

"All sorts of reasons. For example, a few years ago, some random woman sent a movie script she wrote to my agency that she thought I'd be perfect for. No one even mentioned it to me. No one ever read it. It probably got tossed right in the trash. Then, two years later, I did a voice in an animated movie called *Dog Days* about a kid whose mind gets switched with his dog's. The woman's script was about a man who turns into a dog, which is completely different, but still, she went on social media accusing me of stealing her idea. I never heard of her script. I didn't write the movie. But still, she's now telling everyone that I'm the most awful person on earth. And thousands of people are believing her story."

"Oh gosh."

"That sort of thing happens every day. People get angry because you don't want to interrupt your dinner to take a photo with them in a restaurant. Or a barista gets angry because she thinks that because you're famous, you ought to tip her a hundred bucks for a coffee and you didn't. Or a clip of something I said in an interview ten years ago gets posted without any context online in a way that makes it sound offensive, and suddenly a million people are up in arms."

"And you think one of those people might be angry enough to attack your house?"

"*You* were the one who suggested that possibility, not me. But yeah, I suppose there could be a deranged person out there with a grudge against me and a whole lot of dynamite."

Jackson looked a bit scared as he said this, and I actually felt kind of bad for him. Although, it occurred to me that his situation was still better than mine. His house had been damaged, but was still livable—and enormous. Meanwhile, my parents were sleeping in my mother's office because we didn't even have a house anymore. And there were lots of other people on earth far worse off than us.

We arrived at the point where the mansions of the Colony

came to an abrupt stop and the public beach began. It was too early for most beachgoers, but the surfers were out in force. Dozens of them bobbed in the water atop their boards, jockeying for position to grab the perfect wave.

"This is where I usually turn around," Jackson announced. "Want to head back?"

It occurred to me that Sharky might be among the early-morning surfers. He seemed like the kind of person who would be surfing at dawn, and I had some more questions for him.

So I passed on spending more time with Jackson, even though Summer would probably think I was crazy for doing so. "I'm gonna keep going a little farther."

"All right. It was nice talking to you." Jackson started to turn, then thought to add, "And if you *do* figure out there was someone else behind blowing up that whale, besides Chase, let me know."

"I will," I said.

"Good luck, kid." Jackson headed back into the Colony with his bag of garbage.

I continued on, watching the surfers. Most of them were quite good, which made sense; anyone willing to get up so early to do something must have been extremely committed to it. They were a good distance offshore, and with their full-body wet suits to protect against the cold water and their hair slicked back, just about everyone looked exactly the same. I couldn't tell if any of them was Sharky.

As Jackson had said, there were several trash cans on the beach—and despite this, there was still plenty of garbage strewn about. I picked up some more plastic bottles and cigarette butts and tossed them in a can.

Close to shore, two surfers nearly ran into each other on a wave. One was forced to bail out and then got thrashed by the surf. It looked brutal to me, but a few seconds later, she was on her feet in the shallow water. She appeared to be fine—although she was obviously livid at the surfer who'd nearly crashed into her. She shouted a few things that would have gotten me detention in school, then gave him the finger.

The other surfer shouted a few things that were even worse and paddled back out into the ocean.

The girl who'd wiped out plucked her board out of the water and stormed onto the beach. As she got closer, I saw that she was only a few years older than me, maybe eighteen or so, with long hair that was now caked with wet sand. "Did you see that?" she asked me angrily. "That barney totally stole my wave."

"He did," I said supportively, even though I didn't know what she meant. "The big jerk."

The girl laughed at this, then shook off her bad mood. "What are you doing out this way so early?"

"Looking for a guy named Sharky. Is he surfing here today?"

"Haven't seen him. Maybe he's at Leo Carillo. I hear that's running big this morning. Are you his kid? Or his grandkid? Honestly, I have no idea how old that guy is."

"Neither do I. I just met him yesterday."

"Then what do you want with him? Are you looking for surfing lessons? Because I teach. And I usually don't wipe out that bad. That other guy cut me off and I was trying not to T-bone him."

"No, I don't want lessons. I just wanted to ask Sharky some questions."

The surfer gave me a leery look. "About what?"

I hesitated, not wanting to sound as crazy as Sharky, then decided to be honest. "About people stealing sand from the beaches around here."

The surfer stared at me for a moment. I thought she was going to tease me for being foolish. But then she nodded thoughtfully. "That's definitely a thing. My name's Marina. What do you want to know?"

THE SURF RAT

"I've been hearing rumors about the sand thefts for weeks," Marina told me. "But I didn't believe them because, well . . . they seemed ridiculous. I mean, who the heck would steal *sand*?"

We were sitting in the back of her van—which was also her home. Marina was a self-described surf rat. She and her girlfriend drove around the country and surfed, although they occasionally took some time off to do other outdoor activities, like hiking and rock climbing. They had removed the back rows of seats from their van and used the resulting space to store an air mattress, a gas-powered hot plate, a few books, backpacks, climbing ropes, and several cases of ramen noodles. We had the rear doors open and all the windows down, but the van still smelled musty, like damp, unwashed clothes.

"Sorry for the smell," Marina said, not sounding remotely sorry at all. "Sassy and I don't believe in showering. It's a waste of perfectly good fresh water."

Marina didn't smell that bad personally, but then, she had just spent five minutes rinsing the sand out of her hair at a spigot outside the public bathrooms—which sure looked like showering to me, although I didn't say as much.

Marina had pulled off the top half of her wet suit, revealing the swimsuit she had on underneath, but was still wearing the bottom half of the wet suit over her legs, so she looked kind of like a partially peeled banana. She was planning to head back into the ocean after eating breakfast and resting up a bit; she'd been surfing since an hour before dawn. "This beach gets crowded on a good day," she had explained. "If you want to catch some good waves without any competition, you need to be out at first light."

I could see what she meant. Her van was parked along the Pacific Coast Highway, the two-lane road that followed the shoreline from one end of Malibu to the other. Despite the early hour, there were no spaces left. The roadside was lined with a motley collection of vehicles; modified rundown vans like Marina's and ancient cars held together with duct tape were parked among brand new Porsches and Teslas with surfboard racks on top.

"Who have you heard the rumors from?" I asked.

"Other surf rats, mostly. Folks who've camped out at a beach for the night, then woken up to find some of it missing in the morning."

"Camped in a van like this?"

Marina shrugged. "Possibly. Though plenty of folks just lay a bedroll on the sand. It's usually not legal, because, you know, the government would prefer that only rich people get to live on the beach. Like those bloodsuckers." She pointed toward the Colony, using her middle finger to do it. "Sure you don't want any ramen?"

"I'm good," I said.

Marina poked at the small pot of noodles she was heating on her hot plate. She had told me that she and Sassy pretty much lived on ramen, which was about as cheap as food got, although every now and then, they'd go dumpster diving behind a restaurant for leftovers. She didn't seem embarrassed by this at all; instead, she seemed proud of it.

I asked, "Have any of these surf rats heard or seen anything strange?"

"Besides the beach disappearing?"

"I mean like a clue to *how* the beach is disappearing."

"Oh. Yeah. A couple folks have said they heard a weird noise in the middle of the night. Like a machine of some sort. Way offshore, though. Not on the beach."

"And no one saw anything?"

"Not that I know of. But then, I don't know that anyone looked. I mean, you might be too young to have seen any horror movies, but . . . if you hear a creepy noise in the middle of the night, it's probably best to not go hunting for what's making it."

"Even if it seems suspicious?"

"*Especially* if it seems suspicious. Not that anyone imagined it was. They just thought it was a weird noise and didn't realize anything was wrong until they got up in the morning and found half the beach missing."

"Did any of them report this to the police?"

"I doubt it. Do you really think the police would believe someone like me? The moment I'd try to tell them the story, they'd probably bust me for illegally camping."

I decided not to point out that illegally doing *anything* was technically a crime. "Do you know where all this has happened?"

"Mostly around here. County Line. Leo Carillo beach. Topanga. I heard a rumor it had happened up near Santa Barbara, too. And two stoners told me they'd seen it happen in Florida, but they also told me that aliens were behind it, so I take that with a grain of salt."

"And each time it happened here, there was the same noise?"

"Dude, I don't know. It's not like I've been taking

meticulous notes on all this. I've just been hearing that beaches are getting stolen all over SoCal."

"You haven't seen it for yourself?"

"No, but I believe it's happening. I realize Sharky isn't the most rational person in the world. I mean, the guy says he hasn't worn a shirt in ten years. But he knows these beaches better than anyone. If he says someone stole a bunch of sand, then the sand didn't wash away in a storm or drift off in a tide. Someone stole it." Marina turned off the hot plate, then crumbled a handful of salt-and-vinegar potato chips over her ramen. "Adds a little kick," she explained.

Marina seemed to be in awfully good shape, but I wondered how healthy it was for her to live on ramen, potato chips, and scavenged food.

I asked, "Do you know how I could get in touch with some of these other surfers?"

Marina shrugged again, then blew on her ramen to cool it. "Not really. The hard-core surf rats are an itinerant group. A lot of them don't even have phones. Although, if you hang out here long enough, I'm sure Sharky will turn up. He practically lives at this beach."

"Where does he *really* live?"

"No idea. I've never asked him."

Given the way she spoke and the vocabulary she used, I got the impression that Marina was well educated. And yet, she had chosen to sleep in a van and surf every day. "How do you afford to live?" I asked.

Marina laughed. "Maybe you haven't noticed, but this isn't exactly the lap of luxury. It doesn't cost too much to live in a van."

"But it still costs *something*. You have to pay for gas. And ramen."

"True. Sassy and I do odd jobs now and then, build up some cash reserves, then move on to chase the waves. Speaking of which, it's time for me to get back out there." Marina took a gulp of her ramen and hopped back out of the van.

"Already?" I asked, surprised. "You just got out."

"This set of waves won't last all day. And it won't be too long before all the kooks start showing up."

"Kooks?"

"Newbies. People who don't know what they're doing out there and then mess everything up for everyone else." Marina groaned suddenly. "Like this guy."

I climbed out of the van beside her and saw a middle-aged man approaching the road, a shiny new surfboard tucked under his arm. He was heading toward a high-end SUV parked right beside Marina's van, but when he saw Marina, he grew upset.

"You!" he shouted, jabbing a finger toward her. "You nearly killed me out there!"

"You stole my wave!" Marina shouted back. "I had to bail to avoid flattening your dumb butt."

The guy came up to Marina and got right in her face. "That was not your wave. It was mine. I live here, okay? I pay taxes. I contribute to society. And then hundreds of freeloaders like you show up and act like you own the place."

"Get out of my face," Marina informed him. "I have just as much right to be here as you."

"No you don't," the guy said, and then added an extremely offensive insult to the end of the statement.

Marina punched him in the nose.

She obviously knew how to handle herself in a fight. It was a quick, sharp jab. I heard the crunch of cartilage, and then the guy dropped to the ground, cradling his face. "You broke my nose!" he wailed. Although it sounded like "You broke by bose!"

"I warned you to get out of my face," Marina told him, then turned to me. "Guess my morning here is done for. I better split before this jerk calls the cops." She tossed her board into the back of her van and slammed the doors shut.

"Bat's bight!" the guy with the broken nose yelled. "I'm balling the bops!" Although he couldn't call them at the moment, as his phone was still in his car.

Marina hopped into the driver's seat of her van, which wasn't easy given that she still had the top half of her wet suit balled around her waist.

"What about your girlfriend?" I yelled to her.

"She'll figure things out." Marina's casual tone made me think something like this had happened before. "She knows I'll come back for her!"

The van wheezed and coughed as she started it up, and then she peeled out onto the PCH, leaving me behind, standing over the whimpering surfer with the broken nose.

Only a few seconds went by before another car swerved into the empty space, an old convertible with a surfboard jutting out of the back seat, driven by a guy who was thrilled that he'd lucked into such a good spot. "Rock star parking!" he announced. "Score!"

The container for Marina's ramen lay by my feet, the remnants of her breakfast spilled on the ground. She had dropped it while punching the guy and left it behind in her haste to flee. More garbage.

I picked it up and turned to the guy with the broken nose. "Do you need a doctor?"

"Bes I beed a boctor!" the guy yelled at me angrily. "And the bolice! That birl boke my bose!"

I wasn't carrying my phone. So I turned to the guy with the convertible. "Do you have a phone I can use? This man has a broken nose."

The guy with the convertible tossed me his phone, then yanked out his board and his wet suit and hurried toward the beach. "Just put it back in the glove compartment when you're done!" he said.

"You don't want to lock it up?" I asked.

"No time!" he shouted. "The waves are calling!"

I had always thought that FunJungle attracted an unusually strange group of people, but now I was thinking that the residents of Malibu might be even stranger. Or maybe I just attracted strange people wherever I went.

I dialed 911 to ask for an ambulance, wondering if the police would take me seriously if I told them a beach had been stolen.

PUBLIC RELATIONS

"Where have you been all morning?" Summer asked as I came through the sliding glass door from Binka's pool deck.

She was seated in the living room along with Binka, Kandace, and a young woman I hadn't met before. There was a basket of fresh pastries and a bowl of fruit salad on the coffee table, along with cups of coffee and a pitcher of freshly squeezed orange juice.

"Long story," I said.

"Is it about the case?" Summer asked eagerly. "Did you solve it?"

"No. But I found some things out."

"Like what?" Summer seemed desperate to talk about anything besides what was already being discussed in the room.

"There'll be plenty of time to talk to Teddy later," Kandace admonished her. "Right now, we have a guest."

"Teddy, this is Trish Alvarez, my PR rep," Binka said. "Trish, this is Teddy Fitzroy, Summer's"—she paused a moment, wondering what to call me—"friend."

"Boyfriend," Summer corrected.

"Oh," Trish said, as though this didn't seem right to her. But then her consternation faded, and she smiled brightly. "It's a pleasure to meet you, Teddy."

Trish had dressed for work, not the beach. She wore a business dress and four-inch heels that even I could tell were expensive. Diamonds sparkled on her rings and her necklace. Her hair was perfectly coiffed, and her fingernails were long and gleaming. She certainly looked very successful.

"It's nice to meet you, too," I said, fishing a chocolate croissant out of the basket.

Summer said, "Trish was just explaining how I should cash in on my name to earn money."

"Summer!" Kandace exclaimed, looking embarrassed. "Trish never said 'cash in.' She said 'capitalize.'"

"What's the difference?" Summer asked.

Trish perched on the edge of her chair. "Cashing in implies that you haven't done anything. That people will only care about you because you're the daughter of Kandace and J.J. McCracken. But capitalization implies that you have something to offer. That you're more than just an heiress. That you have vision and purpose. Which you do. You have already used your social media assets to make your followers aware of environmental issues, which is a positive thing."

"Yes," Summer admitted begrudgingly.

I knew firsthand that Summer was uneasy about her fame. She had a staggering number of followers, and she was well aware that most of them only cared about her because she was the daughter of a very rich man and a famous model. She had done her best to live life out of the spotlight, foregoing boarding school for public school and never posting anything about her private life—including me. But she also knew that her social reach could be very powerful and, on occasion, she had used it to champion causes that were important to her.

"So all I'm saying is," Trish went on, "why not build on that brand that you've created? For example, I represent an up-and-coming, eco-conscious clothing company that would kill to have you be one of their spokespeople. Now, they can't pay as much as more established brands, but they could offer you a decent fee—and a sizable portion of sales for any of their products that you promote. And the best thing is, it's barely any work at all! Just the occasional tweet or post about how great their products are."

"You mean sell out my values?" Summer asked, aghast. "To a clothing company?"

"An *eco-conscious* clothing company," Trish repeated.

"Come now, dear," Kandace said. "Lots of other people do things like this all the time."

"If this company is so eco-conscious," Summer said, "then why don't they donate their profits to charity instead of paying me to shill their clothes?"

"Because if they don't advertise, then they have no profits," Trish explained. "And then they go out of business and are replaced by some other clothing company that *doesn't* care about the environment. But you can feel free to donate everything they pay *you* to charity." She lit up in excitement at her own idea. "In fact, that would bolster your brand even more. I love it! We can make you out to be some sort of eco-warrior, forgoing your income to save the planet!"

"Ooh! That's smart!" Binka said, then looked to Kandace. "Didn't I tell you Trish was good?"

"So you represent people *and* companies?" I asked Trish.

"I represent whoever wants to enhance their brand," Trish explained. "Big companies, little companies, charities, nonprofits. Actors, models, politicians. I even represent a dog with a huge following on Instagram."

"Which one?" Kandace asked, intrigued.

"Biggles the narcoleptic dachshund," Binka answered. "He's just this dog who falls asleep in funny positions—but thanks to Trish, he has over a hundred million followers!"

"*Two* hundred million," Trish said with false modesty. "And if I can do that for a dog, imagine what I can do for you. Representing individuals as well as businesses is synergistic. If I find that two of my clients have needs that mesh, then I do my best to bring them together. At my company, we're all part of one big family."

"Sounds great to me!" Kandace exclaimed.

"But not me," Summer said, which obviously upset her mother. She looked to Trish. "I appreciate you coming all the way out here, but I'm really not interested."

"Well, perhaps you will be some day soon," Trish said diplomatically. "And as long as you're in town, I thought I might give you a sample of the things I can arrange for you. For example, I have some tickets to the premiere of *Final Glory 4* tomorrow. Would all of you like to go?"

I paused in the middle of grabbing a second chocolate croissant, unable to control my excitement. "A movie premiere? Really?"

"Really," Trish said.

Final Glory was a blockbuster series about a rogue CIA agent who kept getting pulled back into action to save the world. The movies were ridiculous, but also a tremendous amount of fun. The last one had featured a climactic action sequence atop Mount Everest. *Final Glory 4* was coming out the following weekend, and all my friends couldn't wait to see it. My immediate thought was that everyone would be incredibly jealous of us for going to the premiere.

"How did you get passes?" I asked. "Do you work for the movie company?"

"No, but I have friends who do." Trish grinned proudly. "The world of PR is relatively small. I know pretty much everyone in the business in LA, and we all look out for each other. My friends might offer me movie passes or entry into an exclusive club or a weekend at a new casino in Vegas, and I line them up with hot commodities like *you*." She pointed a lacquered fingernail at Summer.

I frowned at the idea of Summer being referred to as a commodity, but she didn't seem to notice. She was now intrigued. "Are the stars going to be at this premiere?" she asked.

"Of course they will!" Trish exclaimed. "And I think you're going to find this event particularly amazing. This movie takes place in the Amazon, so for the after-party, they're going to have all these South American jungle animals, like panthers and monkeys and elephants."

"Elephants?" I repeated, appalled. "Those don't live in South America."

"Really?" Trish asked, surprised. "Are you sure?"

"Yeah," I said. "I'm sure. It's a pretty well-known fact."

"I guess they could have used you on the set of the

movie," Trish said. "Anyhow, it sounds like you're all interested?"

Summer looked to her mother. "Can we go?"

"Of course," Kandace replied. She seemed eager to go to the premiere as well.

"Perfect." Trish plucked a blueberry out of her fruit salad and popped it in her mouth. It appeared to have been the only thing she had eaten. "I'll make sure there are tickets for all four of you tomorrow."

"Awesome!" Summer crowed. "This is going to be the best thing ever!"

"Perhaps not." Trish flashed a coy smile. "There's one other event you might be interested in. The Village Idiots are playing at the Forum tonight."

I wouldn't have thought Summer could get any more excited. But the moment Trish mentioned the Village Idiots, Summer dropped her danish and screamed in surprise. "No way! That's my favorite band!"

"Well that's good to hear," Trish said pleasantly. "Because I have an extra VIP pass to the show."

Summer's elation dropped a notch. "Only one?"

"Yes. Sorry. As you can imagine, it was almost impossible to get them. The show sold out in two minutes. I had to pull every string I could to get the two I have."

Summer turned to me, unsure what to do. I could see that

she would feel bad about going without me to the concert—and yet, it was obvious that she desperately wanted to attend. I wasn't crazy about her leaving me alone in Malibu, but I didn't want to deny her a VIP pass for her favorite band. "You can go," I told her. "I'll be fine."

"You're sure?" Summer asked.

"Sure," I said, doing my best to sound convincing.

"Don't worry," Kandace assured her daughter. "Binka and I will take great care of him."

I pasted a smile on my face. The idea of spending an evening with Binka and my girlfriend's mother felt like it would be extremely awkward.

Summer was so thrilled, she was trembling. She leaped from the couch and gave me a huge hug. "Thank you! You're the best!"

"I know it'll be great," I said gamely.

Summer gave a sudden gasp of alarm. "I don't have anything to wear! I only brought beach clothes!"

"Not to worry, my dear," Kandace said confidently. "Binka and I can help."

"Shopping is my superpower," Binka agreed. "Sounds like a trip to Beverly Hills is in order." She checked her watch. "Although we should go soon. It'll take hours to get there and back, and Summer will still have to dress and then get to the concert."

Kandace snapped to her feet. "Well, what are we waiting for? Let's go!"

Summer turned back to me, looking apologetic once again. "Want to come with us?" she asked, although she already knew what the answer was.

"I'll be okay here," I assured her. I had zero interest in shopping.

"You really are the best," Summer said.

Within minutes, they had hatched a plan for the evening with Trish and were all heading out the door, leaving me alone in the giant house.

Although I should have been happy for Summer, I was bummed. I hadn't even gotten the chance to tell her that I'd talked to Jackson Cross, or to share what I'd learned from Marina. I had been hoping for a day on the beach with Summer, and now she had other plans—while I had none.

I was still standing in the living room, trying to figure out what to do with the rest of my day when Doc entered the house from the casita. He was on his phone, guiding someone back at FunJungle through an examination. "So the abdomen is completely distended? . . . Tender too? . . . She's going to need an operation. . . . No, don't wait for me to get back. I'm going to be here another few days, and this should be done right away. . . . I trust you to handle it. . . . Yes, I mean that. Don't waste any more time talking to me.

Just get it done." He hung up and seemed to notice me for the first time. "Morning."

"What's going on?" I asked.

"Sheba stopped eating. Sounds like she might have an intestinal obstruction."

Sheba was the female Bengal tiger at FunJungle. "Is it bad?"

"She'll be all right. My team can handle it."

This seemed to be further proof to me that Summer was right about Doc's crush on Cass. Normally, he would have jumped on the first plane back to Texas to perform a surgery like this himself. Instead, he was handing it off to his team and planning to stay in LA for a few more days.

"Where's everyone else?" Doc asked.

"Shopping in Beverly Hills."

"Do you have anything to do this afternoon?"

"Nope."

"Well you do now. Cass has a lead in the whale case, and we could use your help checking it out. Oh, and bring a swimsuit. You're gonna get wet."

12

SAND

"Turns out, sand theft is much more common than you'd think!" Cass shouted. "Only, it's been happening in other countries. Not here."

She had to raise her voice to be heard over the roar of the outboard motors. We were in a small, inflatable Zodiac boat, racing across the ocean.

Doc had borrowed one of Binka's many cars, and we had driven down to a place called Long Beach to meet Cass at a marina. Long Beach was still part of Los Angeles, although it was forty-five miles away from the Colony. While there *was* a beach there, it was also home to the second largest container ship port in the United States. Forty percent of all merchandise that arrived in the United States came through it.

It was hard to imagine an uglier stretch of coastline. The

port covered over five square miles, most of which was feature-less flat stretches of concrete. These were filled with labyrinths of shipping containers and parking lots full of semi trucks. The trucks delivered containers full of American-made goods and crops that were heading to other countries, then collected containers full of imports to take back into America. The trucks idled as they waited, belching diesel fumes—and the ships were generally registered to other countries with lax pollution laws. According to Cass, the port had the worst air quality of any place in Los Angeles by far.

The container ships were enormous, a quarter mile long and twenty stories high. Even a blue whale would look puny beside one. It wasn't hard to imagine how a ship so big could have smashed into a whale by accident.

But we hadn't come to Long Beach to see the port. We had come to see the oil rigs.

There were several of them only a few miles offshore. Each pumped crude oil from beneath the seafloor and then shunted it to refineries on the mainland via huge underwater pipes. A local fisherman had told Cass that one of the pipes might be leaking oil. Although other agencies were supposed to investigate such claims, the fastest way to confirm this was for Cass to check it out herself, so she had rented the Zodiac at the Long Beach marina.

We could see the oil rigs from the marina, but they

were still far enough away that it would take us a while to get to them in our small boat, even though it had two 240-horsepower engines. Cass had brought a cooler full of sandwiches and drinks for us, as well as a few fishing rods. "So it will look like we're fishermen and not government agents," she had explained.

"Would it be a problem if the people on the oil rigs knew we were with the government?" I asked warily.

"Possibly," Cass said, and then, before I could ask any more questions, she started to explain what she'd learned about sand. "I tracked down a specialist at NOAA this morning. She told me that sand theft is a growing problem worldwide. Entire beaches and riverbeds have been stolen. People are getting killed over this."

"But why?" I shouted over the motors. "It's just sand!"

"Sand is way more important than we realize," Cass replied. "In fact, these days, it's probably the most import-ant building block of our entire civilization." She pointed to the skyline of Long Beach behind us, a series of skyscrap-ers. "The foundations of all those buildings are made from concrete, as are the highways and that entire port, and the major component of concrete is sand. Every window, auto windshield, lightbulb, and computer screen is made of glass, which is melted sand. And speaking of computers . . ." Cass fished her cell phone out of her pocket. "The silicon chips in this and every other piece of tech on earth are made of . . ."

"Sand," I finished.

"You got it. Sand is also a major component of thousands of other products we use every day: paint, stucco, glue, fiber-optic cables, and even elastic." Cass pointed to the waist of my bathing suit. "Your swim shorts wouldn't be staying up right now if it wasn't for sand. There's no way we can live without it. According to my coworker, we humans use about fifty billion tons of it a year—and we're starting to run out."

"How can we run out of sand?" Doc asked. "The deserts are full of it. The Sahara alone must have a few million square miles of the stuff."

"I asked that too," Cass said. "Turns out, desert sand is very different from ocean sand. Sand in oceans and rivers is actually very rough on the microscopic level, because most of it has only recently been broken down from larger rocks. But desert sand is smooth and round, because it's been eroded by the wind for thousands of years. And when you're making something like concrete, you need the rough stuff, not the round stuff. It's the difference between building a pyramid out of Legos and one out of Ping-Pong balls. One's going to stick together, and the other won't."

I was surprised to hear all of this, and it seemed to be news to Doc as well. "Isn't there also plenty of sand at the bottom of the ocean?" I asked.

"Not as much as you'd think," Cass replied. "Sand tends to be clumped around coastlines, where it's replenished by the erosion of land. Taking it from those areas isn't great for the environment, as it tends to destroy the ecosystem, but we've done plenty of that as it is. In fact, most of the easily accessible sand on earth has already been dredged up. And when you take sand from one place, it tends to affect sand in other places. Plenty of beaches in this region alone are eroding away. Part of that might be due to shifts in climate or weather patterns, but much is probably due to our undermining of sand banks."

I looked back toward Long Beach again. To the south of the port was a long stretch of sand, from which the town had gotten its name. And yet, from our distance, it looked like only a tiny sliver of land. I would have bet that it wasn't anywhere close to fifty billion tons of sand, which meant that humanity would have consumed that beach a hundred times over in a single year. Maybe even a thousand times over.

A few oil drilling platforms sat surprisingly close to the beach—although to make them more picturesque, large fake islands had been constructed to hide the drilling machinery from sight. The islands were constructed from landfill—which was probably mostly sand as well—and then covered with tropical plants.

Meanwhile, the rigs we were heading to had no such

camouflage. As we neared them, I could see why someone would want to shield the ones that were closer to shore from sight. The rigs were basically large factories on raised platforms: ugly blocks of buildings, pipes, and cranes perched atop a network of thick pylons.

And yet, even though it was an industrial facility, there was still plenty of marine life around. Hundreds of sea lions were basking on the breakwater for the harbor, as well as the large buoys that marked the entrance to the shipping channel. Dozens of fishing boats were plying the waters around us, while whale-watching boats crowded with tourists cruised closer to the rigs. Cass had told me that blue whales often fed around the oil rigs, and that dolphins were common as well, although, sadly, we hadn't seen any yet.

"How do these thieves actually steal the sand?" Doc asked. "They must need some heavy machinery to move so much."

"Yes," Cass said. "To get sand from shorelines, they use boats with enormous pumps. They're like a giant vacuum cleaner, for sand. The thieves drop a big hose down to the seafloor and then hoover everything up."

I said, "The surfer I talked to this morning said people had been hearing heavy machinery off beaches during the nights that sand was stolen. It must have been those pumps."

"Makes sense," Doc noted.

"So who do you think is behind this?" I asked.

"Unfortunately, there's a long list of possibilities," Cass replied. "It could be a concrete manufacturer that wants cheap supplies, or a company that makes glass or silicon chips or paint or any of a million other products—or a developer who wants cheap landfill."

Doc sighed. "So once again, we have a crime being committed by big business."

"Most likely," Cass agreed. "There's not many individuals who would need that much sand—or have the ability to move it."

"What about a family like the Dermans?" I suggested. "They obviously have plenty of money. What if the mountain was eroding under their giant mansion and they needed extra landfill to support it?"

"I'm sure the Dermans could afford to buy all the landfill they need," Doc said dismissively.

"Maybe not," Cass countered. "If I had a dollar for every high-flying billionaire out here who turned out to secretly be bankrupt, *I'd* be rich. And often, what puts them in the hole is building one of those mega mansions. Maybe they cut some corners in its construction and now their ten-million-dollar guesthouse is about to slide down the hill. So they're illegally shoring it up."

Doc immediately abandoned his argument. "Good

thinking," he told Cass, even though I was the one who'd raised the idea in the first place.

A cruise ship was passing to the west, heading for Long Beach as well, although there was a much nicer docking area for it than the container ships. Even though it was at least a quarter mile away, it was still staggeringly large, a floating skyscraper fifteen stories tall. I wondered how many tons of sand had gone into all the windows, paint, and other materials on that ship alone.

Then something else occurred to me. "If a container ship could kill a whale by running into it, then so could a cruise ship, right?"

"That's true," Cass said thoughtfully. "Plus, a cruise ship company would probably be even more concerned about its image—and they have plenty of money. I can easily imagine one of them blowing up a dead whale to get rid of the evidence that they'd killed it."

"The cruise ship industry doesn't have a great environmental record," Doc added. "There's been plenty of incidents of ships flushing waste and dumping garbage at sea. Maybe one of them took a shortcut through a protected marine life area and hit the whale."

The GPS unit on the boat suddenly pinged, indicating we'd reached the coordinates Cass had plugged into it. She quickly cut the motors, and we glided to a stop.

Without the roar of the engines, it was extremely quiet out on the ocean. We were miles from the traffic and bustle of the city. Save for the slap of waves against the pontoons of our Zodiac, the only sounds were the faint hum of other boats in the distance and the occasional clang of the bells in the channel buoys.

"This is the spot my friend said he'd seen oil in the water," Cass announced. "More or less."

"Out here?" I asked. "We're still pretty far from the rigs."

"The pipelines pass right under us, though," Cass explained. "Most of them were only expected to last twenty-five years but have been in constant use for twice that long. So it wouldn't be a surprise if one of them has broken down. Or maybe a container ship dropped an anchor on one."

I leaned against one of our boat's inflatable pontoons and peered over the edge into the water. I had been expecting a big, obvious slick of black goo, but the water looked fine to me. "I don't see anything," I reported.

"The leak might not be so evident from the surface." Cass opened a large chest she had brought along. It looked like a fancy tackle box, but inside was an array of test tubes and chemicals. "We'll need to take water samples from a variety of depths." She checked the depth finder. "Looks like the floor is a hundred and fifty feet below us. So let's sample every ten feet here, then try a few more spots in the vicinity.

Although first, let's make ourselves look like harmless fisher-men." She picked up one of the rods, expertly cast the line, then set the rod in a special holder in the stern.

Doc and I also cast lines. There was no need to put bait on them, since we weren't really trying to catch anything. Then we got to work.

To take the water samples, Cass had a specially designed device: a long shaft that she could lower test tubes into the ocean with and control when the stopper was removed from each. We had to load each tube separately, lower it to the desired depth, fill the tube, bring it back up, and carefully mark it so that we didn't get all the samples mixed up. The work wasn't difficult, but it was monotonous, and now that we weren't moving, there wasn't much of a breeze, so it got hot quickly. Our small boat had no shade, and the sun was baking us.

We had been taking samples for about thirty minutes when I heard a distant roar of excitement. It was coming from one of the whale-watching boats, about a half mile away from us. All the tourists were crowded on the bow. As I watched, I saw a spout of water erupt in front of the boat. There was another roar as all the tourists cheered at once.

"There's a whale!" I exclaimed.

Cass had seen it too. "A blue," she said knowingly. "And a big one, given the size of that spout."

"Can we go see it?" I asked.

Cass gave me an apologetic look. "We have work to do, pal. And I'm on the clock. I can't spend the day chasing whales, no matter how much I want to."

I looked to Doc, hoping he would overrule Cass, but he obviously didn't want to do anything to upset her. "Sorry, Teddy. But this is important."

I groaned, making my annoyance obvious. Nothing seemed to be going my way. First, my home had burned down, and now my California vacation wasn't working out the way I had hoped. I'd been roped into solving a new mystery, my girlfriend was going to a concert without me, and so far, the only whale I had seen up close had exploded. The fact that there was another whale nearby, but I couldn't go see it, was incredibly frustrating. "Please?" I pressed. "Just for a few minutes?"

"I wish we could," Cass said. "But by the time we get over there, the whale will probably have sounded, and it could be another twenty minutes until it comes up again. We need to get this work done while we're here."

"I agree," Doc said, although I sensed that, deep down, he really wanted to go see the whale himself.

Despite their insistence that we had to work, Doc and Cass were obviously distracted by the whale in the distance— as was I. In fact, we were so focused on it, we didn't notice the speedboat approaching until it was almost beside us.

It was built to go fast, with an aerodynamic wedge shape and two 350-horsepower engines in the back. The hull was weathered and scarred, but the engines looked relatively new. Four fishing rods were set up in the stern, but no one was using them; the lines weren't even out. Three big, muscular men were aboard.

The one driving had a sleeveless T-shirt that had once been white, but was now so stained with grease that it was almost black. He called out to us as he came closer. "How's the fishing over here?"

The other two men were wearing jackets over T-shirts, which was odd for a hot day out on the water. They smiled, but something seemed forced about it.

I noticed Cass's guard was up too. "Not so good," she said. "We were just about to move on and try somewhere else."

The speedboat pulled up alongside us, with its bow facing our stern.

"What's going on there?" the driver asked, pointing to the chest full of test tubes. He sounded friendly, but there was an edge to his voice. "That doesn't look like you're fishing at all."

"Doesn't look like you are either," Doc observed.

"Oh, we're fishing all right," the driver said, more

menacing now. "And I think we might have caught something. What agency are you with? The EPA? NOAA?"

Cass did a good job of acting confused. "What are you talking about?"

"Or are you one of those activist groups?" the driver went on. "Like Surfrider or Heal the Bay? Are you looking to cause some trouble?"

"We're just fishing," Doc insisted. "If we were with the government, do you really think we'd have brought a kid out here?"

"All right," the driver said with a sigh. "I tried to be nice about this, but you're still lying to me. So let's do it the hard way."

The other two men withdrew guns from beneath their jackets and pointed them at us.

"Hand over the water samples," the driver said.

THE CHASE

Now that I knew the men wanted our samples, it was obvious that they had come from an oil rig.

In addition to the driver's shirt, there was grease all over their clothes, the result of working with machinery. The men also had the big, sinewy builds of people who did hard labor. Someone at the rig must have spotted us poking around the area of the oil leak and dispatched the toughest, least morally conscious workers they could find to steal the samples from us.

The moment I saw the guns, my heart leaped into my throat, but Cass and Doc remained surprisingly calm. Both of them kept up the charade of being normal fishermen.

"Easy now," Cass said. "These water samples aren't for

any government agency. They're only for us. To help us locate the fish."

"I don't care what you say they are," the leader of the men snarled. "If you don't hand them over, we're gonna feed you to the sharks."

I turned to Cass, concerned. "That's a *really* good argument. Maybe we should just do what he said."

"I agree," Doc said, eyeing the men cautiously.

Cass gave Doc a look of betrayal, but then nodded agreement. "All right. I see your point." She turned her attention to the case full of samples, but instead of lifting the entire thing up to hand over, she only picked up one test tube. It was empty, but she clutched it in her hand to hide that from the men. "This is the most important one," she informed them. "So I guess you'll be wanting it first?"

"We want *all* of them," the leader said.

"And you'll get them," Cass told him. "But you need to be *really* careful with this one. Because the liquid inside is explosive."

"Explosive?" one of the gunmen asked worriedly. It was the first time he had spoken, and his tough facade now cracked in concern.

"*Very* explosive," Cass warned ominously. "Catch!" With that, she tossed the test tube onto the other boat.

She threw it perfectly, into the space between all three of the men, just far enough away that none of them could actually reach it.

The men responded in different ways. The leader dove to catch it. The two gunmen tried to escape the blast. One hit the deck, curled into the fetal position, while the other leaped overboard into the water.

The empty test tube shattered harmlessly in the speedboat. But it had done exactly what Cass had hoped, distracting the thugs from pointing their guns at us.

Cass immediately leaped to the stern of our Zodiac and fired up the engines. We took off so fast that Doc and I were thrown off our feet; we quickly left the other boat behind.

Although we weren't out of danger yet.

Behind us, the two men who were still in the speedboat helped the one who had jumped overboard clamber back in. Their boat was facing the wrong direction, but it didn't take them long to turn it around and come after us once again. Their motors had more horsepower than ours, which meant we wouldn't be able to outrun them. The safety of shore was too far away, and there was nowhere to hide out on the open ocean.

Doc seemed to have the same concerns as I did. "Why didn't you just hand over the samples?" he yelled to Cass over the roar of the motors. "We could always come back for more!"

"Now that they know we're onto them, they wouldn't let us come anywhere near that pipeline again!" Cass yelled back. "Plus, that test kit is really expensive! Speaking of which, Teddy, can you lock it up tight so that nothing gets broken?"

With our boat jouncing over the waves, the test tubes in the kit were rattling like seeds in a maraca. A few had even shimmied out of their holders and were rolling around on the rubber floor of the Zodiac. I was getting rattled a lot myself. It was impossible to stand in the juddering boat, so I had to crawl across the floor to collect the loose tubes and place them in the kit.

Doc shouted to Cass, "This is still risky! Those guys had guns!"

"They were only trying to scare us!" Cass said dismissively. "There's no way they'll shoot us over a few water samples."

A gunshot rang out.

Cass gulped. "Although I guess I could be wrong about that."

I turned from securing the kit to look behind us. The speedboat was gaining on us, skimming across the water like a skipped stone, while our little craft was getting pummeled by the waves.

Doc and Cass were seated on the pontoons, clutching safety ropes to keep from being bounced overboard. Doc looked to Cass, obviously worried. "Er . . . you *do* have a plan here, don't you?"

"More or less," Cass replied, with far less confidence than I'd hoped. She pointed ahead of us. Instead of heading to shore, we were heading toward the whale-watching boat. "I figure, if we can get close enough to them, those guys will back off. They're not going to shoot us in front of witnesses."

"You thought they weren't going to shoot us, period!" I reminded her.

Cass didn't reply to that. Instead, she warned, "Hold on!"

We soared over the crest of an extremely large wave, and, suddenly, there was nothing beneath us. I slammed the lid shut on the test tube kit, then clutched the chest tightly to keep everything inside—and to prevent myself from being tossed into the ocean. We slammed back down onto the surface of the water so hard, it felt as though I'd been punched.

Another shot rang out behind us.

It occurred to me that maybe the gunmen weren't shooting at *us*. All they had to do was hit one of the inflatable pontoons. If it burst, our boat would be out of commission—and the bad guys would have no trouble recovering the water samples. But while being stranded out in the middle of the ocean was much better than being dead, it still was a fate I hoped to avoid.

I locked the lid onto the kit and scuttled to the side of

the Zodiac, where I could grab on to the safety rope as well.

The whale-watching boat was now much closer to us—but that wasn't only because we were racing toward it. The whale boat was also coming toward *us*. I could now see that it was a large, motorized catamaran, supported by two large hulls that held the body of the boat four feet above the water's surface. It was designed for maximum viewing, with six rows of tiered seats at the bow, as well as a viewing deck atop the main cabin. Despite all the seating, most of the tourists were on their feet, crowded along the railings, clutching binoculars and cameras with telephoto lenses, keeping their eyes peeled for whales—although many of them were now watching us. Dozens of people pointed in our direction, seeming to realize something was wrong.

And yet, even as we neared them, the speedboat didn't back off. Instead, it bore down, quickly gaining ground on us. I could see the guns of the thugs in the bow, glinting in the sun.

Cass attempted some evasive maneuvers, jigging the Zodiac back and forth, but those only made us wet and nauseated while the speedboat kept on coming. It wouldn't be long until it was right alongside us, and we'd be easy pickings.

"Cass," Doc said firmly. "These samples aren't worth dying for!"

"I still think I can shake these guys!" Cass insisted.

"How?" Doc demanded.

"I'm working on it!" Cass replied.

The whale-watching boat was now only two hundred yards away from us. I suddenly realized something important—something that I probably should have thought of much earlier. (Although, in my defense, there was a lot going on.) If the tourists were coming *toward* us, there was probably something luring them that way.

I scanned the surface of the water ahead of our boat.

Halfway between us and the whale-watching boat, the ocean suddenly bulged. The waves broke apart as something enormous rose beneath them.

"There's a whale right in front of us!" I screamed.

A second later, the whale surfaced.

Only, it didn't look like a living thing to me. It was simply too big. The dead whale in Malibu had been bigger than any animal I had ever seen—and yet, it was nowhere near the size of the animal in front of us. I felt as though I was watching a submarine emerge—or perhaps an undiscovered land mass. There was a huge, sleek expanse of grayish-blue skin, which rose to a small, rounded peak that looked oddly like a giant human nose.

This was the whale's blowhole, and as it came to the surface, two massive geysers of water burst from the nostrils, shooting thirty feet into the air.

A chorus of cheers went up from the tourists—as well

as several worried gasps from people who had just realized what I had:

We were on a collision course with the whale.

A blue whale can swim as fast as thirty miles an hour, which is disturbingly fast for an animal the size and weight of a ten-story building. Meanwhile, we were going even faster in the opposite direction, and the speedboat behind us was going faster yet.

The speedboat was nearly beside us, with the thugs aiming their guns our way. The driver yelled something that we couldn't possibly hear over the noise of all the engines. Probably another threat to turn us into shark chum.

Cass immediately took action to avoid the whale, veering sharply from its path.

We managed to barely miss it, cutting right in front of the blowhole, on a route that took us directly over the whale's colossal head. We passed so close to the whale's nostrils that I could hear the rush of air as it breathed in, and then we were racing alongside the great length of its spine, close enough that I could have reached over the edge of our Zodiac and touched it.

It was at once amazing and terrifying to be so close to such a monumental living creature. I felt like a flea beside a dog, aware that if the whale were to swat us with one of its fins, it could crush us. But it was impossible to tell if the whale even knew—or cared—that we were there.

It was hard to imagine that anyone could be so close to something so big and not even notice it—and yet, somehow, the driver of the speedboat had done just that. Apparently, he was so focused on us that the whale escaped his attention until it was too late. He had stayed right behind us and now found the great bulk of the whale suddenly looming in his path. He swerved to avoid the beast, glancing off the blowhole, which provoked an angry snort from the whale in response.

The reason that a blue whale's blowhole looks vaguely like a nose is that it basically *is* a nose, albeit one on top of the whale's head. It connects to the whale's windpipe, which leads directly to the whale's lungs, allowing the whale to breathe without coming very far out of the water. Toothed whales such as orcas only have one nostril, but baleen whales, like blue whales, have two, which makes the blowhole even more noselike. The lungs of a full-grown blue whale are each the size of a school bus, holding over 1,300 gallons of air, which can be forced out at speeds of over three hundred miles per hour. And because the blowhole serves the same function as a nose, the spray that comes out of it isn't only water—it's also mucus. So when the whale snorted, it blasted the speedboat and the bad guys with a tremendous amount of whale snot, which hit them at high speed and slimed them from head to toe.

That would have probably been disgusting enough to put most people out of commission, but the whale wasn't done with the thugs yet.

While the gunmen were reeling from being coated with mucus, their boat careened along the length of the whale's back. We were slightly ahead of it, on the opposite side of the whale's spine. As we neared the rear end of the whale, the beast dove. Its locomotive-size head sank into the depths, while its tail lifted out of the water directly ahead of us.

Compared to the tails of other whales, a blue whale's isn't very attractive. It doesn't have big, wide flukes like a humpback, which needs them to launch itself out of the water to breach, or a sperm whale, which uses them to propel itself fast enough to catch prey like giant squid. Instead, the blue whale's flukes are small in relation to its body, so the tail looks rather stubby. But up close, it was evident that the tail was incredibly thick and powerful, like a sequoia tree made out of muscle.

We shot right by it without incident, but as the speedboat passed, the whale gave its tail a slight twitch, the way a horse would to flick away flies. Only, in this case, the whale flicked away the speedboat.

I suppose this could have been an accident—although it seemed to me that the whale did it on purpose, as if it was annoyed at the speedboat for bumping into it. Whatever the case, the effect was just as devastating. The speedboat was tossed aside like a bathtub toy. The three thugs tumbled into the sea while the boat itself cartwheeled through the air and landed bow first in the ocean so hard that it broke apart.

On the whale-watching boat, the tourists gasped in amazement.

The enormous tail plunged into the water behind us, leaving a huge spot devoid of waves known as a footprint. But after a few seconds, even this vanished, and there was no sign at all that the largest animal on earth had just been there.

Cass, Doc, and I were so riveted by the whale and what it had done to our pursuers that we forgot to watch where *we* were going until we heard the screams of the tourists. We wheeled around to see that we were now about to plow into the whale boat itself.

"Get down!" Cass ordered.

We all dropped to the floor of our Zodiac. Rather than trying to avoid the catamaran, we simply went right under it, threading between both of its hulls. The four feet of space between the floor of the main cabin and the surface of the ocean was just big enough for us. We made it through with only an inch to spare, then shot out on the other side, leaving the startled tourists and the thugs from the oil rig behind.

Now that no one was chasing us anymore, Cass let off on the throttle. The Zodiac slowed and stopped jouncing on the waves, which allowed us all to stand again, although I still felt like my legs were made of rubber.

Doc got to his feet, staring at Cass the whole time. For a few moments, I thought he was going to chastise her for recklessly endangering our lives.

But instead, he burst into laughter.

In all the time I had known him, I had never heard Doc laugh like this before. It was a deep, booming chortle that rang across the water, and Doc was laughing so hard, he could barely speak. "That was . . . ," he gasped between breaths, "absolutely . . . incredible! . . . I've seen . . . some wild things . . . but never anything . . . like that!"

Before I knew it, I was laughing too. And so was Cass.

"That whale sucker punched those jerks right out of the water!" Cass snickered.

"And it snotted them too!" I added.

"It sure did!" Doc crowed. "With probably twenty pounds of mucus each!"

"Serves them right!" Cass cried.

We all sank back down onto the pontoons, laughing hysterically.

And then my phone started buzzing in my pocket.

We had just come close enough to shore to get cell

service, and hundreds of texts were coming in at once.

We hadn't been out of range too long, so receiving that many texts seemed odd to me.

I took out my phone to check them.

The first I saw was from Xavier. Dude. What's up with you and Summer?

The next were from our other close friends Dashiell, Violet, and Ethan, who all seemed concerned.

I had to scroll through the texts quickly to figure out what everyone was talking about.

Xavier had included a link with his original text. I clicked on it.

What I saw made me feel as though *I* had been swatted by the tail of a blue whale.

I immediately stopped laughing.

The link connected to a tabloid website that posted photos of celebrities.

The top photo was of Summer. And she was kissing the lead singer of the Village Idiots.

THE VICTIM

I was so upset, even a pool full of baby sea lions couldn't cheer me up.

Although the thugs from the oil rig were out of the picture, Cass and Doc had figured it still wasn't safe to return to taking water samples. The people on the rig knew what we were up to and would most likely send someone else out to threaten us, and this time, we might not get away. Besides, we had collected thirty-two samples, which Cass thought might be good enough. So we returned to shore and went our separate ways. Cass headed to a lab to get the samples tested, while Doc finally got around to visiting the wounded sea lion he had come to California to see. I joined him.

The sea lion was being treated at the Los Angeles Marine Mammal Care Center, which was only a few miles from

Long Beach. Our route there took us directly through the port. Dozens of cargo ships were being unloaded by the huge cranes, while semi trucks waited in mile-long lines for their turn to haul the containers out one by one.

The Care Center was located only a few blocks from a bluff that overlooked the Pacific. It was designed very simply; eight pools were enclosed by chain-link fences and shaded with tarps strung above. Each pool was twelve feet square, twelve feet deep, and filled with seawater. There were a few harbor seals at the Care Center, although most of the inhabitants were sea lions. A volunteer had told me that all the animals there had been found stranded on the beaches, primarily due to illness, injury, or malnutrition. The Center's goal was to rehabilitate them and release them to the wild again, which they managed to do with most of the animals they rescued.

The sea lions were separated by age. The youngest were only a few months old, most having recently been weaned off their mothers' milk. At the Center, they were well fed and cared for, so they were healthy and rambunctious. They were adorable, with big dark eyes and stubby flippers, gleefully plunging into their pool and hopping back out again, chasing one another about and, once they were finally exhausted, collapsing to rest together in piles of bodies.

Doc had gone off to check on the sea lion that had been

blinded, leaving me to watch the youngsters. Normally, I would have been charmed and amused by their antics, but not that day.

Summer had kissed someone else.

The kiss obviously wasn't romantic. Summer was merely giving the singer a peck on the cheek, the same way she would greet Dash or Ethan or Xavier when she saw them. The singer's name was Wynn Gyoko, and Summer was a huge fan of his. It appeared that she had gone backstage to meet him before the show and given him an excited, but chaste, kiss. However, social media was making it out to be something much more serious. The internet was blowing up, reporting that Summer McCracken had a new boyfriend.

Wynn was only a year older than Summer, just like the other members of the Village Idiots, but despite his young age, he was staggeringly rich and famous. I didn't pay much attention to pop culture, and even I knew that Wynn had had a string of relationships with young actresses and other singers. Now everyone was presuming that Summer was next on that list.

As was often the case with social media, much of what was being reported was completely wrong. People were claiming that Summer had been spotted at many of the Village Idiots' previous concerts that summer, or had already gone on many clandestine dates with Wynn, none of which was true. But seeing my girlfriend being linked to such a well-known and successful young heartthrob was still distressing.

Although the thing that *really* upset me was that Summer hadn't responded to any of it yet. She hadn't denied any of the stories—and, even worse, she hadn't responded to me personally. It was possible that she hadn't noticed the story was trending at first, but I had written to her several times about it, and I was sure that many of our mutual friends had too. I hadn't heard a thing from her. Which meant Summer was avoiding me.

I didn't want to think that Summer was ditching me for Wynn Gyoko, but with every minute that elapsed without a call or message from her, I got more and more distraught. After all, Wynn was handsome, successful, rich, and famous, whereas I was none of those things.

At the far end of the Care Center, Doc was examining the blind sea lion. It was a medium-size male, not quite mature yet. The volunteers at the Center had trained it to come to the side of its pool so that it could be cared for in return for a fish. It was there now, its head out of the water, mouth wide open and ready for food, while Doc knelt down and peered into its eyes. Finally he nodded and said something to the volunteer behind him, who tossed a fish directly into the sea lion's mouth. The sea lion immediately slipped back into the water with its prize and swam away.

From what I could tell, the sea lion didn't seem very

hampered by its blindness. If I hadn't known it couldn't see, I wouldn't have been able to tell that was the case.

My phone buzzed in my pocket. I took it out excitedly, hoping it would be Summer.

Instead, it was Xavier. My heart sank a bit, but I was still glad to hear from a friend.

"Hey," I said, answering it.

"What's going on out there?" he asked breathlessly. "Have you heard from Summer yet?"

"No."

"What? Why not?"

"I don't know. The concert doesn't start till later. Maybe she's still hanging out with the band."

"Oh," Xavier said, sounding worried.

"Oh what?" I asked.

"Nothing," Xavier said quickly. "I'm sure everything's fine. What's all that barking in the background? Are you at a dog park?"

"They're not dogs. They're sea lions. Doc brought me to the Marine Mammal Care Center."

"Whoa. That sounds awesome. What are you doing there?"

It seemed to me that Xavier was trying to change the subject, but I wasn't going to let him do it. "You said 'oh' like you were worried. What are you worried about?"

"I'm not worried about anything," Xavier said, but he was obviously lying.

"Just tell me what you're thinking."

Xavier hesitated a moment, then said, "You promise you won't be upset?"

"I promise."

"Well, it's just that Summer's not from the same world that we are. I mean, she *acts* like she's one of us, but she's not. She has more money than everyone else at school put together. I work at FunJungle; she *owns* it. It's like she's a lioness and we're all impalas. Or dung beetles. And . . . well, people say things. Not to *you*. But they say them."

"What kind of things?"

"Just like, wondering if she's ever going to get tired of living out in the sticks with us and go back to her old life. I mean, she used to go to boarding school and hang out with other rich kids all the time, and then she stopped. Maybe she misses it. You guys haven't even been in LA two days, and she's already hanging out backstage with Wynn Gyoko. That sort of thing doesn't happen where we live. The closest thing we have to a celebrity at FunJungle is a person who dresses up like a hippopotamus. Know what I mean?"

"Yeah," I said sadly.

Xavier was absolutely right: Summer and I were from very different worlds. If the McCrackens ever wanted to ditch Texas and buy a multimillion-dollar beach house in the Colony, they could do it without any trouble at all. Whereas I had grown up in a tent camp in Africa and now lived in a trailer park. Or rather, I *had* lived in a trailer park. I didn't even know where I was going to live when I got back to Texas. Summer had everything she could possibly want, whereas, after the fire, I had almost nothing except the clothes I was wearing. Summer fit in in Malibu; I didn't.

So maybe it was only a matter of time before Summer realized that a person like Wynn Gyoko would understand her better than I did. Or, at the very least, as Xavier had said, maybe she would decide that small-town life was too dull for her and leave me behind.

A few seconds passed. Then Xavier asked, "Are you angry? You said you wouldn't be angry."

"I'm not angry. I'm just bummed."

"There's a good chance all this stuff isn't even true. It's just what some people have been saying—and let's face it, a lot of the people we go to school with are dimwits. The fact is, Summer's obviously crazy about you. She wouldn't have invited you to Malibu with her if she wasn't."

"And then she went to the concert without me."

"Did you tell her that you were okay with it?"

"Uh . . . yeah."

"Well, then you can't be upset at her for it. If you got

invited to the Super Bowl without her, would you go?"

"Sure, but . . ."

"But nothing. You'd go."

"If she's so into me, then why hasn't she called me?"

"I don't know. Maybe her phone is off. Or the battery died. Or the reception at the arena stinks. There's a lot of possibilities."

Doc was coming toward me, passing down the corridor between the enclosures. The young sea lions all hopped out of their pool and waddled to the fence, barking hungrily, obviously hoping that he was bringing food. Doc barely seemed to notice them. He was reading something on his phone. Then he looked up at me and signaled it was time to leave.

"I gotta go," I told Xavier.

"Okay," he said, then quickly added, "I'm sure you don't have anything to worry about with Summer!" Although it didn't sound as if he fully believed that himself.

"Thanks," I said, then hung up.

Doc made a beeline for the parking lot without even saying a word to me. Now that he wasn't around Cass, he was back to his usual gruff behavior.

"What's wrong?" I asked. "Is it the sea lion?"

"No," he replied. "The sea lion's as healthy as can be, given what happened to him. He wouldn't be able to survive in the wild, but he'll do perfectly well at FunJungle. I'm having the pinniped department make arrangements to transfer him."

"So then what are you upset about?"

"I just heard from Cass. She already had the water samples tested. Turns out, there is an oil leak at that site."

"Oh. And that's bad for all the wildlife there?"

"Yes. But the leak isn't as big as we thought it might be. Oil is leaking into the water, but not nearly enough to kill an animal the size of our whale."

"So the oil company wasn't responsible?"

"No. As far as our mystery is concerned, we're back to square one."

15

FISH

We had intended to head straight back to Malibu, but the return route was a dark red line on the GPS system, which estimated that it would take two and a half hours. It appeared that every single person in Los Angeles had decided to go for a drive at the same time.

"Beach traffic," Doc explained. "It's hot inland, so everyone heads to the water."

He decided to change our plans. Instead of taking the crowded highway, Doc looped around the Palos Verdes Peninsula on a lonely road with gorgeous views of the ocean until we arrived at a beach community that looked as though it had been forgotten for decades. There, he parked at a nondescript mini-mall and led me into a tiny restaurant with Japanese writing on the windows. Inside, there were only three tables and a sushi bar.

We sat at the bar. I started to grab a menu, but Doc shook his head and pointed to a sign on the wall that said TRUST ME. Then, to my astonishment, he spoke to the sushi chef in Japanese.

The chef brightened considerably, and they spoke back and forth for a minute. Afterward, the chef went to work with renewed vigor.

"You speak Japanese?" I asked Doc.

"Apparently so," Doc said, making me realize that I had just asked the dumbest question of all time.

"Since when?"

"College."

"And how did you know about this place?"

"I used to be the head vet down in San Diego," Doc reminded me. "I had some friends up this way. They turned me on to this spot long ago. You're in for a real experience."

A waitress came over, bearing bowls of warm edamame and miso soup. I had eaten both before, but only rarely; sushi was expensive, and the closest Japanese restaurant to my home in Texas was over an hour away in San Antonio.

Doc fell silent for a while, so I did too, not wanting to ask any more dumb questions. I focused on trying to dislodge the edamame from their pods, but I wasn't so good at it. I kept squeezing too hard, making the beans fire out and carom off the soy sauce bottles.

After a while, I reached for my phone to see if I had somehow missed a text from Summer.

The moment I had it out of my pocket, Doc snatched it from my hand. "Don't keep checking," he said, setting the phone beside him. "Just enjoy the meal."

"But what if she texted . . . ," I began.

"Then she can wait for a response." Doc took a sip of his soup, then sighed. "Women. They can really drive us crazy, can't they?"

"Yeah," I agreed.

"We need to figure out what happened to this whale."

I understood there was more to that thought. Doc wanted to solve the mystery to impress Cass. Although he certainly cared about bringing the criminal to justice as well. "Cass is sure that that oil leak couldn't have killed the whale?"

"She sounded awfully convinced."

"Because the whale we saw today seemed to be spending a lot of time near the oil rigs. If there's oil leaking there, even only a little bit, couldn't it build up in the whale's system over time?"

"Cass didn't seem to think so. She says you'd need a much bigger slick to impact a whale."

"So what happens to the oil company? Will they shut the rig down until they fix the leak?"

"Ideally. Although they'll probably do everything they can to stall the process. I mean, they obviously knew about the leak already. But instead of dealing with it, they were covering it up. That's why they tried to run us off and steal our samples."

"Why not just fix it?"

"It's expensive to shut down the rig and do repairs. And it's bad public relations to reveal that the pipes are leaking."

"Wouldn't it be worse to reveal that there was a leak, but they covered it up?"

"Yes. But then, they obviously weren't planning on us finding out."

"Well, if that pipe was leaking and no one was doing anything about it, couldn't there be another rig with a leak somewhere close by that no one knows about?"

"I suppose. There's still a good amount of rigs operating off the coast of California. And even more down in Mexico. Well in range for a blue whale."

"And we can't possibly check them all," I said, resigned.

Doc shook his head. "There's probably fifty miles of pipelines, and it's all under at least a hundred feet of water."

I popped some edamame into my mouth, thinking

about how difficult this mystery was to investigate. Even a young whale could travel hundreds of miles in a day, far more than most adult land animals, which meant that it might have been exposed to whatever had killed it far away from where it had ultimately died. Meanwhile, the ocean currents moved things all over the planet; a toxic chemical spill could have happened in one place, poisoned the whale in yet another, and then drifted on to somewhere else. Finally, it was difficult to know what was happening more than a few feet below the surface of the ocean. If the blue whale we had encountered that day had been twenty feet farther down, we would have passed right over it without even knowing it was there. My father had once pointed out to me that land animals were limited to moving about on the surface of the earth, while marine life had the entire ocean, which meant that 99.9 percent of all livable area on the planet was underwater. Trying to deduce what had occurred in all that space was a daunting task.

The sushi chef placed two bowls on the bar in front of us and said something in Japanese. Doc responded in the same language, actually sounding nice, and then slid one of the bowls in front of me.

Inside were a few slices of raw fish in a watery brown sauce. I poked at them warily with a chopstick. On the few occasions that I had eaten sushi before, I had never seen anything like this.

"Try it," Doc told me. "You'll be glad you did." He deftly plucked a piece out of the bowl with his chopsticks and popped it into his mouth.

I wasn't nearly as skilled with my chopsticks. I made several attempts to pick up the fish, but it was slippery and skittered around in the bowl. Finally I gave up on the traditional method, used one chopstick as a tiny harpoon, and speared a piece.

It was one of the most delicious things I had ever tasted. I groaned with delight. "What is this?"

"Yellowtail in a homemade ponzu sauce. Told you you'd like it." Doc picked up another piece to eat, but then froze, staring at it.

"What's wrong?" I asked, worried. "Is the fish bad?"

"No. I just remembered something that happened when I was working in San Diego: a sushi restaurant around here got busted for serving whale meat to its customers."

"Ugh. Who would want to eat whale?"

"There are plenty of people who'd ask why anyone would want to eat raw fish. Or ground meat patties with melted cheese and ketchup. Or peanut butter and jelly, for that matter. Different cultures like different things. In many parts of Europe, they eat horse. In other parts of the world, they eat dog. Here, we find the idea of that disgusting—but we're more than happy to eat pigs. Although, as I recall, most of the patrons at the restaurant didn't actually know they were eating whale. The owners were claiming it was another type of meat entirely—until they got busted in an undercover sting by US Fish and Wildlife."

"And you think someone might have been trying to kill a blue whale for the same reasons? That'd be enough sushi to feed all of Los Angeles."

"That's probably not likely. However, I'll bet there's a good chance the whale was killed by a fishing boat. It's something we failed to discuss with Cass before. Commercial fishing is extremely poorly regulated. It's almost impossible to oversee. I've heard estimates that there might be upwards of three million fishing boats active on earth, and there's almost no funding to police them. Plus, every country has its own laws—and once you get out into international waters, everything changes."

"Three million fishing boats?" I repeated. "But most of those must be small, right? Too small to kill a whale?"

"Even a relatively small boat can trawl with a really large net. And trawling snares millions of unintended marine animals."

"I've heard of that. It's called bycatch, right?"

"Exactly. It's hard to get accurate statistics, but I've heard estimates that over three hundred thousand whales and dolphins are killed as bycatch every year. Not to mention millions of sharks, sea turtles, and who knows what else. Mostly, those would be smaller animals, which was why I didn't think of it before, but I suppose there's a decent possibility that even a juvenile blue whale could get snared in a big enough net."

"But there weren't any signs that the whale on the beach had become entangled, were there?"

"I didn't notice any, but then, we weren't there very long before the whale was blown up. Which certainly destroyed any evidence there might have been," Doc said.

"Good point."

"Although you're right. It's probably much more likely that a big fishing vessel would be needed to harm a whale. These days, there are corporate fishing boats that are basically floating slaughterhouses. Some are almost as big as container ships, and they're putting out nets or fishing lines that can be miles long. Or they're bottom trawling, which involves dragging a weighted net along the seafloor and scooping up everything in its path. That's like bulldozing a forest. It's feasible that one of those methods could accidentally kill a whale."

I polished off my yellowtail, although it no longer tasted quite so good, given our subject matter. "Do you think this fish was caught using any of those methods?" I whispered, so the sushi chef wouldn't overhear.

Doc cautiously considered his last piece. "I don't know," he admitted finally. "These folks have always claimed to only serve sustainably harvested fish, but that's probably hard to verify. Although *this* is definitely environmentally friendly." He brightened as the sushi chef set another set of small plates in front of us.

Whatever was on them was not fish. Instead, there were lumps of orange goo. And it smelled funny.

"What is this?" I asked worriedly.

"Sea urchin. It takes relatively little resources to raise them on farms, and even when they're caught in the wild, that's not necessarily a bad thing. Since we've wiped out so many of their predators, urchins are overpopulating and destroying ocean environments like kelp forests. So you can absolutely feel good about eating this."

I cautiously poked at my orange goo with a chopstick, wary of eating it. But if it was a sustainable seafood, then it seemed as though I should give it a try. And besides, Doc had already wolfed his down and seemed to be enjoying it.

I put the whole thing in my mouth. Which was a mistake.

I didn't like the taste, but I liked the texture even less. It had the consistency of paste—and the adhesiveness as well. I couldn't swallow it. And I couldn't spit it out, because the sushi chef was looking at me expectantly.

"Do you like it?" he asked.

I made the most positive-sounding noise I could, despite the mass of goo in my mouth, then gulped some water, hoping that would help things. Eventually, I managed to chew up the urchin and swallow it.

The sushi chef grinned at me and went back to work.

Doc gave me a wry smile. "Not a fan, huh?"

"Not really," I admitted.

"Maybe you'll like it better next time. It grows on you."

"So does foot fungus. But I'm not about to eat that."

Doc laughed. "All right. We'll be a little less adventurous. No more sex organs of echinoderms."

I felt myself turning green. "Those were sex organs?"

"Yes."

"Why didn't you tell me?"

"Because then you never would have tried it."

I gulped more water and swished it around, trying to get every last remnant of sea urchin out of my mouth.

I wished I had liked it more. I looked over all the fillets of fish in the refrigerated case of the sushi bar, wondering how many of them had come from sustainable methods and how many had been caught by the sort of factory ships that might have killed the whale.

Which got me thinking about the mystery again. "Suppose our whale did get killed by a net or a fishing line? Is there any way that could be tracked back to the ship that used it?"

"Possibly," Doc answered.

"So it would definitely make sense that they'd want to get rid of that evidence."

Doc arched an eyebrow, intrigued. "A big fishing ship shouldn't even be working anywhere around here. Those operations are restricted in the waters off California. But that doesn't mean such a ship wasn't doing it illegally. If it was, then getting a whale ensnared in their gear would be doubly incriminating."

"Is there any way to track fishing ships like that?"

"There must be." Doc took out his phone and started searching.

The sushi chef set two more small plates in front of us. Each had what appeared to be a piece of fish perched atop rice, but I still hesitated before eating it. "This is just fish, right?" I asked Doc. "Not urchin gonads or sea slug turds or anything like that?"

"It's just fish," Doc assured me. "Mackerel, to be exact."

I ate mine. It was delicious.

"There's a *lot* of ship tracking sites," Doc reported. "Let's try this one." He brought it up on his phone.

A map of the planet appeared with every large ship marked on it. My immediate reaction was shock.

The symbols were obviously not to scale, so the ships appeared larger than they would have been in real life, but still, the amount of sea traffic was startling. The main routes of maritime traffic were so busy that they looked like high-ways on a car's GPS system. Thick lines of ships crisscrossed the planet—although there were plenty of vessels almost everywhere outside the arctic regions. The symbols were color coded to represent different types of ships; altogether, it looked like a tub of confetti had been spilled all over the earth.

Doc slid my phone back to me so that I could explore the same site simultaneously. I noted, to my annoyance, that Summer hadn't texted yet, but I was too focused on investigating to dwell on this.

Doc and I quickly worked out the color-coding system. Oil tankers were red. Cargo vessels were green. Fishing vessels were orange. Cruise ships were dark blue. Big yachts were pink. Large passenger ferries were yellow. There were also plenty of "unspecified craft" that were gray.

Some areas of the world had significantly more marine

traffic than others, and of different sorts. The eastern coast of Asia was thick with container ships, while oil tankers were clustered around the Middle East and the gulf coast of the United States. Cruise ships and luxury yachts were more likely to be in the Mediterranean and the Caribbean— although there were plenty of other vessels in all those places as well. I could click on any one of them and get all sorts of information on the ship, such as its name, destination, and even a track of where it had been over the past few days.

There was so much to sort through that several more courses of sushi had been served before I even got around to focusing on Los Angeles.

Dozens of container ships and a few oil tankers were packed around the port of Long Beach, while many others sat in the channel between the mainland and Catalina Island. Doc presumed most of those were waiting for a chance to unload at the port.

The number of large fishing vessels in the area was much smaller. But there were still quite a few, along with several cruise ships and yachts. "There's an awful lot of ships big enough to harm a whale around here," I noted.

"There are," Doc agreed. "And to make things worse, there's also a chance that the ship responsible isn't nearby anymore. Maybe it was headed out to sea when the incident happened, rather than heading to port."

"How far away could a ship get in that time?" I asked.

"Let's see." Doc did a quick Google search on his phone. "Looks like a big ship can move at around thirty miles an hour. That's over seven hundred miles a day. The whale washed up on the beach four days ago, but it might have been wounded as much as a day or two before that. If we consider that it's six days . . ." He did some math, then sighed heavily. "Then the ship could be over four thousand miles away by now. That's over halfway to Asia. It could be just about anywhere in the Pacific."

I considered the tracking app on my phone. "There are hundreds of ships within that range. Maybe thousands."

Doc checked his own phone to confirm this. "Yeah," he said, sounding as daunted as I was. "There's a lot of them, all right."

"Do you think there's any way to narrow that down?" I asked hopefully.

"I don't know. And even if we could . . ." Doc trailed off sadly.

"What?" I asked.

Doc took his time before answering, as though trying to decide how much honesty I could handle. "I'm not sure that we'd be able to do anything."

"Well, maybe not us, but Cass might know someone at a government agency that could inspect the ships or something like that."

"I wouldn't count on that happening."

I sagged on my bar stool. "Why not?"

"Like I said, hundreds of thousands of dolphins and whales are killed by the fishing industry every year—as well as millions of other marine creatures. The agencies that police this sort of thing are stretched thin as it is. I doubt they can allocate so much time and resources to solve the death of just one whale."

"But there's obviously something important about this whale. Because someone blew it up to get rid of the evidence of their crime."

"I know. Which is why I'm not giving up on this. I want to find out who did this and bring them to justice as much as you do. But it's not going to be easy. And . . ." Doc hesitated once more. "There's a chance we won't succeed. Or that, even if we do figure out who did this, they'll get away with it anyhow. For example, if the ship that did this turns out to be from another country, we might have very few options to prosecute them."

The sushi chef slid two more plates of food to us. This time, it was lump crab meat and rice, wrapped in cones of dried seaweed. Normally, I would have been excited to eat it.

I love crab, and ever since the sea urchin, the food had been delicious. But I had lost my appetite. I now felt depressed about the mystery, daunted by our dim prospects for solving it—and guilty about all the fish I had eaten. My concerns about Summer returned as well. All those things combined to give me a big stomachache.

And my evening was only going to get worse.

THE FIGHT

The traffic was still bad after dinner, so it took Doc and me nearly two hours to get back to Malibu. Doc called Cass to share our idea about the fishing industry being involved in the death of the whale. Cass appreciated it but echoed the very same concerns that Doc had about what a long shot it would be to investigate any ships at all. At the end of the call, Doc seemed frustrated. Without a solid new lead in our case, he was running out of excuses to spend time with Cass. He shifted back into his usual, grumpy self, and we spent the rest of the drive in uncomfortable silence.

I still hadn't heard one word from Summer.

She wasn't back from the concert yet when Doc and I finally returned to the beach house. Binka and Kandace weren't there either; they had left a note saying they were out to dinner with friends. Doc went off to the casita. I took a shower and called home. Dad had already left for Argentina, but Mom was eager to know what I had been up to that day. Once again, I left out a few of the events. I told her about seeing the blue whale and the Marine Mammal Care Center, but not about the gunmen coming after us. I regretted this even as I was doing it, but I didn't want Mom to be upset. Lying to her only made me feel worse. Plus, I missed her and was feeling lonely. Being in the big house all by myself made me even more annoyed at Summer for ditching me that night.

I decided to do some more research on the ship-tracking app to distract myself, but the phone service in Malibu wasn't great, and I had neglected to ask Binka for her WiFi password. So I went searching for a computer I could use instead.

Binka's house was so large, there was still plenty of it that I hadn't seen. For example, the whole top floor. Binka's bedroom was directly above mine, and Summer had told me that her closet alone was bigger than the entire FunJungle koala exhibit. It didn't seem right to go up there without permission, though. I checked out all the other guest bedrooms, some of which seemed as though they might not have been used in months, if ever. There was also a home gym, a screening room, a sauna, and what appeared to be a room just for getting massages. None of these had computers in them.

And then I found an entire floor I hadn't even known existed.

It turned out the house had a basement level. It wasn't as though it was hidden; Binka simply hadn't mentioned it. It was accessed by an unassuming door in the front hallway. I had presumed the door only led to a closet but was stunned to discover a flight of steps leading down.

Binka hadn't said it was off-limits, so I went to explore.

The basement level appeared to have been Roswell Crowe's private space. There was a pool table, a bar with beer taps built in, and several leather couches that did not seem to be in Binka's style arranged before a large-screen television. The walls were decorated with dozens of framed photos of Roswell standing next to famous people: actors, singers, politicians, and athletes. Many of them were taken at construction sites, indicating that those people might have been clients whose homes Roswell was building. The room certainly wasn't being used much. It had a musty smell, indicating it hadn't been aired out recently, and there was a light film of dust on everything. The only item that looked like it had been used at all since the divorce was the dartboard, which now had a photo of Roswell tacked over the bullseye; several darts jutted out of his forehead.

More things that belonged to Roswell were piled haphazardly atop the pool table, as though they had been purged from the rest of the house and dumped down there. It seemed that Roswell hadn't gotten around to collecting them yet— or perhaps Binka hadn't let him take them.

There was a box with more framed photos, ones that I assumed had once been on display elsewhere. These featured Roswell and Binka together. Although Roswell was much older than her, he appeared to be in good shape. One photo from their wedding day had a spiderweb of cracks in the glass over Roswell's face, as though someone had punched it—or maybe thrown something at it.

There were also lots of men's clothes, a large humidor full of cigars (although all of them had been snapped in half) and a lot of stuff from Roswell's business: boxes full of contracts and tax returns, a few hard hats, and a great number of rolled-up blueprints.

There was no computer that I could use.

I turned my attention to the blueprints instead.

Each roll was clearly marked with the name of the project. I quickly came across several names I recognized. Roswell Crowe had done work on the homes of Hrishi Argawal and Wes and Nancy Smith, all of whom Jackson Cross had mentioned to me, as well as Jackson himself. I also found blueprints for the Buckinghams, the Dermans, and plenty of famous people. It seemed as though Roswell had built or remodeled half the houses in the Colony.

I looked back at the pictures on the wall. Sure enough, in many of them, Roswell and the owner were standing on the beach with the construction project behind them.

Roswell had built houses other places too. I found plans for mansions in the hills of Malibu, Beverly Hills, and Bel Air. He had even done some work for Skip Howell, the head lifeguard, building an extra bedroom onto his house. A handwritten Post-it note on the plans for Skip's house said, *Don't charge Skip for anything but expenses.—R.C.*

I unrolled the blueprints for Jackson Cross's home. That one had been built from scratch. The plans detailed an enormous primary bedroom suite, a "restaurant-class" kitchen, a wine closet, multiple guest rooms, a five-car garage, a home gym, a screening room, two casitas, the infinity pool, and a dredged-out basement just like the one I was standing in.

Most of the other homes had relatively similar layouts. Everyone seemed to want the same types of rooms, and since the properties were so narrow, there was a limited way to arrange them. It made sense that the primary bedroom and the main living space would all be on the beach side, while rooms that didn't require a view, such as the gym, screening room, or garage, would all face the street.

I did find the occasional personal touch. The Dermans had an entire racquetball court inside their home, Hrishi

Argawal had a theme park–style waterslide for his pool, and the Buckinghams' home was designed with turrets— apparently so they could refer to the place as Buckingham Palace. (It was referred to this way on all the plans.)

But the most intriguing item was in the Smiths' home. Off their basement, dug into the earth beneath their garage, was a large room simply marked on the plans as *arsenal*. Jackson Cross had told me there were rumors the Smiths had made their money from arms dealing, and this seemed to confirm it. The room had exceptionally thick walls and an elevator from the garage to access it. There was no way for me to tell if the room was to store weapons for the Smith business—or if it was merely a personal arsenal—or if maybe the room had some other purpose entirely that I didn't understand. But still, it was odd to see in someone's beach house.

I was flipping through other drafts of the Smith blue- prints, hoping to find more information about the arsenal, when I came across a blueprint for another project entirely. I figured that, maybe, Binka hadn't taken much care to keep everything organized while moving Roswell's stuff into the basement. This blueprint wasn't for a house at all. Instead, it was for a large seaside shopping center named Surfside in a place called Redondo Beach. The project involved build- ing a pier, a parking garage, a small theme park, and over a hundred thousand square feet of shops and restaurants.

Much of the garage was going to be underground and the pier was going to need huge pylons sunk into the ocean floor to support the weight of a roller coaster, a Ferris wheel, and assorted other park rides. None of those were going to be nearly as elaborate as the ones at FunJungle, but still, I suspected the pier would need to be extremely sturdy to hold them. The whole thing looked to be quite an undertaking.

I shifted my attention to the boxes filled with contracts, interested to learn more about the project. It turned out that an entire box was devoted to Surfside alone. The contracts were all over a hundred pages long and filled with legal jargon that I couldn't make sense of; they might as well have been written in another language. They were all dated from over five years before. Mixed in with them were several thick environmental reviews that had been conducted by various federal agencies. These were equally incomprehensible, although this time, they had been written by engineers, rather than lawyers. From what I could tell, the government did not appear to be in favor of the project. There were concerns with things like "dense nonaqueous phase liquids," "hydraulic gradients," "permeable layer failure," and—most disturbing of all—"activated sludge." On one report, in the same handwriting that had been on the contract for Skip's house, someone had written some very nasty things about the chief geologist.

I dug farther into the box, trying to learn what had ultimately happened with the Surfside project, but before I could find anything, I heard noises upstairs. The walls of the basement were so thick they muffled the sound, but I knew Summer's voice well enough to recognize even a faint trace of it.

It was now 11:30 p.m. I quickly replaced the contracts, rolled up all the blueprints, put everything else back where I had found it, and hurried up the stairs.

I emerged from the basement to find Summer at the front door, waving good-bye to Trish as she drove away. She was dressed in her new clothes and still had her VIP pass from the concert on a lanyard around her neck. Despite the late hour and the fact that she'd been out all day, she was full of energy. The moment she saw me, she grinned from ear to ear.

"You're still up!" she exclaimed. "Thanks so much for letting me go tonight! It was the best night ever! I met Wynn Gyoko! And everyone else in the band!"

"I know," I said brusquely. I had hoped to keep my annoyance in check, but it came out anyhow. "The whole world knows. Everyone thinks you're dating him."

Summer rolled her eyes. "This is why I hate the internet. It's always wrong. Want something to drink? I'm sooooo thirsty." She headed into the kitchen.

I followed her, feeling even more annoyed by how quickly she had brushed off my concerns. "Why didn't you text me back?"

"About the whole Gyoko thing? Because it's no big deal."

"It is to me! You were kissing him!"

Summer paused with the refrigerator open, seeming to realize how upset I was for the first time. "It was just a little peck on his cheek. That's all. The same thing a million other fans have done to him."

"Well the million other fans didn't have the internet say they were a couple."

"Welcome to my life." Summer took a can of flavored water out of the fridge and cracked it open. "I've had a run with no stories like this for a few months because I've kept out of the public eye, but there were plenty before I met you, and I promise, there's going to be plenty more after this."

"So why don't you do something about it?"

"Like what?"

"Deny that you're dating him! And tell everyone that you're dating me instead!"

Summer laughed, like this was ridiculous. "No one would ever believe it."

"You could at least try."

"Trust me, Teddy, you don't want that."

"How do you know what I want?"

"It's no fun, being in the public eye all the time."

"Really?" I snapped. "Because it looked like you were having plenty of fun with Wynn Gyoko."

Summer gave me an icy stare. "You don't have any idea what it's like, being me. I'm not just getting linked romantically to every famous person I meet. I'm constantly getting judged. And mocked. And degraded. By millions of people I don't know. People call me mean or fake or dumb or say that I'm ugly. For every nice thing that gets said about me, there's a thousand mean things. I'm just trying to protect you from all that."

"Well it feels like you're embarrassed to admit that you're dating me."

"And it feels like you're just jealous of Wynn."

"Why shouldn't I be? You're not afraid to post photos of kissing *him* for the whole world to see."

"I didn't do that!" Summer snapped. "Someone else did! This is exactly what I'm talking about. Any other teenager could kiss Wynn and it'd be no big deal, but I do it and suddenly the whole world's acting like we're going to get married."

"If you're so concerned about it, then maybe you shouldn't do something dumb like kissing Wynn in front of the cameras." I knew what I was saying was hurtful, but I was too angry to stop it.

Summer recoiled at the word "dumb." "It was just one little kiss, Teddy. I didn't do anything wrong."

"You ran off to a concert and left me alone while we had a mystery to solve. I thought you cared about that."

"I *do* care about it."

"It sure doesn't seem like it. Doc and Cass and I nearly got killed today while all you did was snuggle with Wynn Gyoko."

Summer stared at me. I thought she was going to say something nasty back to me, but then I noticed she was crying. "Just so you know, Wynn *did* ask me to go on a date with him. But I said no. Because I *thought* I had a nice, understanding boyfriend. I'm not happy that this happened. I wasn't trying to hurt your feelings! But now, it sure seems like you're trying to hurt mine. I'm going to bed." She stormed past me and headed up the stairs.

I watched her go, not knowing what to do. Part of me wanted to apologize—while part of me was angry at her for not apologizing about kissing Wynn. And then not texting me all night. Even though I knew it was probably wrong, I let my anger dictate my behavior. I just stood there silently, until I heard Summer's bedroom door slam shut.

Summer and I had never had a fight before. Sure, we'd had disagreements, or hadn't seen eye to eye about a few things, but there had never been anything like this.

I went back up to my own room, feeling more miserable than I ever had in my life, and wished that I'd never agreed to come to Los Angeles.

EAVESDROPPING

I tried to go to bed but was too amped up to sleep.
I was agitated after my fight with Summer, and my mind was filled with questions about all the mysteries at hand.

What had killed the whale? A ship strike? A fishing net? An as-of-yet undiscovered oil leak? A chemical spill? Or had the whale merely fallen victim to some of the tons of plastic that everyone on earth had allowed to get into the ocean? Whatever the reason, someone was concerned enough about it to destroy the carcass to hide the evidence and frame someone else for the crime. What could possibly have driven the culprit to such extremes? And how would we ever find them?

So far, we had almost no evidence to go on, thanks to the demolition of the whale. Investigating the few leads we had was going to be exceedingly difficult—if it was even possible at all. This was certainly the most daunting crime I had ever faced.

Although the mystery of the stolen sand was also troubling. In that case too, there were few clues, short of the accounts of two surfers, neither of whom seemed completely reliable. So who was behind the thefts—and what were they doing with the sand they were stealing? And how was I supposed to catch someone who was operating all over the coast of Southern California when I couldn't even drive?

After more than an hour of lying in bed and wrestling with my thoughts, I gave up and went out onto the balcony to look at the ocean, hoping that would calm me down.

To my surprise, I discovered I wasn't the only one who was still awake.

Kandace and Binka had finally returned from dinner and were splayed out on chaise lounges on the pool deck below me, drinking wine and chatting. In Texas during the summer, it would have been warm and humid, even in the middle of the night, but it was chilly by the beach. Both of the women were wrapped in thick robes, and I could hear the hum of electric heat lamps around them.

There was also a strong breeze coming off the water. It made the night even colder—although, on the plus side, it also whisked away any lingering dead whale odors. Instead, the air smelled fresh and clean.

Between the lamps and the roar of the surf—and the fact that both women appeared to be a bit tipsy—neither of them heard me emerge onto the balcony. Meanwhile, they were speaking in the slightly-too-loud tones that drunk people sometimes use, which carried up to me.

"It *is* lovely out here," Kandace was saying, slurring her speech a bit. "This view is to die for—and if we were back home, the mosquitoes would have sucked us dry by now."

She was right on both counts. It was a relief to be able to go outside without slathering on bug repellent—and even at night, the view was great. A half moon had risen, and the foam of the surf glowed beneath it. In the moonlight, I could see the silhouettes of a few boats. Three were anchored about a hundred yards offshore, while one was not far off the beach around the point where the dead whale had been. None of them had any lights on, so I couldn't tell if they were fishing boats or yachts.

"You can't really be happy out there in the sticks, can you?" Binka asked. "It must be so dull."

I was expecting Kandace to defend her decision to live there. Instead, to my dismay, she said, "It *is*. When the only culture you have is the musical numbers at the dolphin show, that's a problem."

Binka giggled, then asked point-blank, "Then what are you still doing there?"

"It has its charms. The people are lovely. I enjoy riding my horses. . . ."

"There's plenty of places to ride horses around here. And the people aren't so bad. Most of them, anyhow."

"What am I supposed to do, leave my family behind?"

"No! Bring them! J.J. is powerful enough to work from anywhere. . . ."

"He'll never leave Texas. . . ."

"Then let him stay. He can jet back and forth whenever he wants."

"And Summer would kill me. She really likes her school. And her friends. And, of course, there's Teddy."

"Teddy?" Binka spoke with the same tone that she might have if Kandace had just said that Summer liked cockroaches. "What does she see in that boy?"

"Teddy's as sweet as they come," Kandace said in my defense. "And he's *very* smart. He has a real gift for solving mysteries. . . ."

"Seems more like a gift for sticking his nose where it doesn't belong. Jasper Wingate down the beach says some kid was snooping around on his property early this morning and described Teddy to a tee. He was very upset about it."

"I thought you said Jasper Wingate was a world-class dirtbag."

"He's also one of the biggest producers in Hollywood. I

don't want him angry at me for hosting riffraff at my house."

I clutched the railing tightly, upset by the way Binka was talking about me. I hadn't even met Jasper Wingate, although I remembered Jackson Cross mentioning him. If he lived near Jackson, then the "snooping" he was accusing me of was actually me picking trash off the beach in front of his home. Not that he had bothered to check for himself.

I wondered if the real reason Jasper didn't like me poking around his property was that he had something to hide.

Meanwhile, Kandace obviously wasn't pleased by the way Binka was talking about me either. I could hear it in the tone of her voice. "If Teddy was poking around Jasper Wingate's property, I'm sure he had a good reason. He was probably trying to figure out what happened to the whale."

"We *know* what happened to the whale. It beached itself, and then those fools Chase and Scooter blew it up as a gag. The police say the case is cut and dried."

"Teddy obviously doesn't think so. And neither does Summer."

Binka snorted with disdain. "You see what I'm talking about? That boy is a bad influence on your daughter. Maybe, back in Texas, it's fine and dandy to let children investigate crimes, but here, we let the police do it. Teddy needs to back off and mind his own business."

"Oh come now. He's not causing anyone any harm."

"What if he upsets more of my neighbors? These aren't like the people you live near. They're *important*. Movie directors and music producers and agents and people like that. If one of them gets angry at me, they could ruin my career like that." Binka snapped her fingers. "Everyone in the Colony is already worked up because of this exploding whale. Windows have been broken. Pools need to be drained. There's whale guts and seagull poop everywhere. Lola Ray, the rapper, has to repaint her entire house—and she just had it done three months ago. She's furious. So if some little busybody starts going around accusing people of murder, it's going to cause problems. I need you to talk to that boy and make him stop."

Kandace didn't answer for a few moments. Finally, she said, "All right. I'll talk to him—but under one condition."

"What's that?"

"I don't want you saying anything else nasty about Teddy in front of Summer. No calling him 'riffraff' or a 'busybody' or anything like that. She likes him."

"But she could do so much better for herself. Trish says that Wynn Gyoko was crazy about her. . . ."

"Don't get me started on Trish. She's the one who spread that rumor about Summer dating Wynn, isn't she?"

"Did you see how many followers Summer picked up once it hit? At least half a million, just in the past few hours. I told you Trish was good."

"I thought her job was to make Summer money, not tell lies about her."

"The more followers you have, the more money you make. That's how the world works these days. I wouldn't be surprised if, by tomorrow morning, there's a dozen companies clamoring for Summer to promote their products. Maybe more. I'm telling you, Trish is a gem. She's brilliant at her job—and she's always hustling. Twenty-four hours a day, seven days a week. I don't think she sleeps. You need to hire her for both you and Summer. Before you know it, you'll be swimming in cash."

"I already have more money than I know what to do with."

"Money that J.J. earned, not you. You ought to build up a nest egg in case things don't work out in the long run."

Kandace gasped. "Now you're telling me to leave J.J.?"

"No. I'm just saying it could happen. Because it happens all the time. You might finally decide Texas is too dull for you and leave him behind. Or J.J. might do the leaving. I mean, I never thought Roswell would ditch me, but he did. For a woman less than half his age, that skunk. Although I'm getting this house and half of everything he owns, so . . . win-win, I guess." Binka held up her wineglass in a mock toast and then drained it. "Looks like I'm empty. Want some more?"

"I think I've had enough," Kandace said. "I'm wiped out and I'm cold."

"Poor thing. Your blood's gone thin living in hot, sweaty Texas. I can turn the heater higher."

"No, I think it's time for bed." Kandace got back to her feet, which took a surprisingly long time. "Oh boy. That last glass of wine was one too many."

"Lightweight," Binka chided, even though she was having the same problem. It looked like the two of them were trying to stay upright on a rocking ship, rather than solid ground. Finally, Binka managed to steady herself—and then walked right into the sliding glass door.

Kandace tittered. "You did that exact same thing back when we had that shoot in Paris. . . ."

"As I recall, *you* were the one who walked into the glass door. I fell down the stairs because of those ridiculous six-inch stiletto heels they made me wear." Binka fumbled with the door, trying to get it open.

"Remember the photographer on that shoot? Jasper Wingate reminds me of him. A total sleazebag."

"Oh, Jasper's not that bad. The media always makes him sound like a huge jerk, but he also . . ."

I didn't hear the rest, though, because Binka finally managed to open the door and they both slipped inside.

While I was disappointed to miss the rest of this story,

I was happy to head back indoors. I hadn't brought a robe or a blanket outside, so I was freezing. My bare feet felt like blocks of ice. I leaped back into bed and balled up under the covers, trying to get warm again.

Although now I had even more questions than before.

In particular, I couldn't help but be bothered by Binka's professed concern for her neighbors. Was that the real reason she wanted me to back off investigating the dead whale? And if not, then what was?

SHARKY

"I know who blew up the whale," Sharky told me.

It was the next morning, and once again, I had come down to the surfer beach.

As I had passed Summer's bedroom, I had thought that I heard her stirring and considered telling her where I was going, but then decided against it. I knew that not inviting her along was petty of me, but I was still upset with her. It was possible that she was still upset with me, too, and I didn't want to have another argument. All that had left me feeling confused and lonely as I walked along the beach.

Marina's van was parked along the PCH again, in almost the exact same spot it had been the morning before. I had sat on the sand nearby, watching the surfers, planning to catch Marina or her girlfriend when they returned and ask them if they'd heard any more about the sand thefts.

But Sharky had come along first. He emerged from the waves, sheathed in his wet suit, carrying his board and stopping every now and then to cock his head sideways and shake it to clear the seawater from his ears. I reminded him that we had met two days before, right before the whale had exploded, and said I wanted to talk to him more about the sand thefts. He was excited to hear that, although first, he wanted to discuss the whale.

That was fine with me. Sharky was odd but seemed well attuned to what was happening in the area. After all, he had recognized that sand was being stolen when others hadn't. So maybe he had noticed something important about the dead whale as well.

"Who did it?" I asked.

"The government."

I frowned. "Why would the government blow up a whale?"

Sharky gave me a disappointed look, as though I was terribly naive. "Dude, the government is behind *everything*. You know how, down in San Diego, the navy has trained dolphins and sea lions to detect old mines and torpedoes and stuff like that?"

"Yes." As bizarre as this sounded, the stories were actually true. Because of their great ability to sense things underwater, trained dolphins and sea lions were better at finding undetonated explosives than humans were.

"Well, for years, I've figured the navy was also training whales."

"To find mines?"

"No! Submarines! I mean, a whale and a sub are about the same size, right?"

"I guess."

"So not only can the whale *find* the subs, but they can take them out, too! Like, if a full-size blue whale rammed a sub . . . boom! No contest. But you can't train a whale the same way you train a dolphin, so the government has to use mind control."

"Mind control?" I repeated, now thinking that maybe Sharky had seawater not just in his ears but also in his brain.

"Exactly! They have to get them young, right? About the same age as the one that washed up on the beach. Because when they get too big, they're dangerous. And then the feds implant stuff in their heads to control them. But something obviously went wrong with this one. Like its circuits shorted and it went haywire and beached itself. And the government didn't want that researcher lady to cut it open and find out about the program. So they blew up the whale."

"Hmmm," I said. I didn't believe Sharky's theory at all, but it occurred to me that if *anyone* was capable of blowing up a whale, it was the military. The armed forces certainly had access to explosives that most civilians didn't. And the navy had plenty of ships big enough to kill a whale by striking it. Or perhaps some military division had accidentally shot the whale. It could have been during a training exercise—or possibly the whale had been mistaken for an enemy craft. I wondered if the military was just as worried about bad public relations as a private company might be—and how far they would be willing to go to cover up their mistakes.

"Or maybe," Sharky continued thoughtfully, "the government wants the whales to be an army against the megalodons."

"I thought megalodons were extinct."

"No way. They're out there, all right. But the government's keeping their existence a secret. Just like they do with UFOs."

"Why wouldn't the government want us to know about megalodons?" I asked.

"The government doesn't want you to know about *anything*. Not space aliens or megalodons or teleportation or whatever else. Everything you think you know is only what they *want* you to think you know."

I tried to wrap my head around that last sentence but couldn't. "What?"

"The government is always trying to manipulate things

behind the scenes. Like, for years, they've been trying to get us surfers off this beach so they can turn around and sell all the land to the Richie Riches so they can build even more of those mansions." Sharky pointed accusingly toward the Colony.

"But didn't the government set this beach aside as a park in the first place?"

"Yeah, but not for surfers. They probably wanted to build a navy base here, or something like that. But then all the billionaires were like, 'No way! We want to put up more mansions!' And the government does whatever the billionaires want, right? So now they're trying to get rid of us."

"How?"

"They're always spying on us. Look!" Sharky pointed to some people walking along the beach. It was an older couple in loud matching Hawaiian shirts and flip-flops.

"I think those are just tourists," I said.

"Or maybe government agents in disguise. See? They're taking pictures!"

"That's also what tourists do."

"Dude, you can't be so complacent. The government doesn't want you to question anything. Which is why I question *everything*. I don't have a phone. Or a credit card. Or a driver's license. Because the government uses that stuff to keep tabs on all of us."

A thought suddenly occurred to me. "Do you think the government is tied to the theft of the sand, too?"

"Nah. Not *our* government, at least. Our government wants to keep the sand here. Because the billionaires want beachfront property."

"Then what government do you think took it?"

"Dubai, maybe. Did you know they built these huge fake islands there for more billionaires to live on? Some are shaped like palm trees—and others are shaped like a map of the world."

"I've heard of that," I said. Even though this sounded like another crazy idea of Sharky's, it was the truth. Sharky obviously read the news on occasion. The fake islands were regarded by many scientists as an environmental disaster, as they had been built atop coral reefs and other natural habitats.

"I hear they ran out of sand," Sharky reported. "Because even though Dubai's in the desert, they wanted beach sand for the fake beaches. Not desert sand. So they've been stealing it from other places all over the world."

"Hmmm," I said again, unsure whether or not to take this seriously. After all, Dubai had gone on a massive building spree in recent decades, creating a city out of almost nothing within a relatively short time. In addition to the fake islands, the country had also constructed other outlandish things, such as the world's tallest building and an indoor ski mountain—despite the fact that it was often over 120 degrees there in the summer. All that construction would have required a massive amount of sand—as would other huge projects in cities all over the world, now that I thought about it. If countries could send fishing trawlers to illegally ply the coasts of other places, why couldn't they send dredging boats to steal sand?

Sharky suddenly reeled as though he had been punched in the face.

"Are you all right?" I asked.

"I just realized something!" he exclaimed. Apparently, when Sharky had a big idea, it literally almost knocked him off his feet. "Maybe the whale was part of the government plot to take this beach away from us. Like, they were going to send whales in with mind control to mess up the surfing. Or maybe have them beach themselves here so that they'd rot and get all stinky and gross so no one would want to surf here anymore. But they got their coordinates wrong and the whale ended up on the beach at the Colony instead. What do you think?"

"Er . . . ," I said, trying to avoid saying what I *really* thought, which was that Sharky had definitely fried too many brain cells over the years. Luckily, Marina emerged from the surf and saved me.

"Hey!" she said upon seeing me. "How's it going?"

"All right," I answered.

"Is Sharky telling you one of his crazy theories? Like how Atlantis used to be located off San Diego?"

"I never said that!" Sharky snapped, sounding offended. "I said it was off *San Francisco*!" He looked to me and lowered his voice in confidence. "I know a guy who's seen the ruins. But the government had megalodons patrolling the area to keep anyone from finding it."

"Whoops." Marina looked to me apologetically. "Didn't mean to get him started."

"You laugh now," Sharky told her. "But you won't be laughing when I'm proved right and get the Nobel Prize for Discovering Stuff."

"Speaking of which," Marina said to me quickly, obviously trying to change the subject, "I got some more info for you. Though I need to eat. I'm starving. Want some ramen?"

"I'm fine," I said, not wanting to take any of her food.

"I'd love some!" Sharky said, even though Marina hadn't asked him.

Still, she didn't complain. "Sure thing," she told him, then led the way toward her van.

"Did you get into any trouble yesterday?" I asked.

"Nah. In fact, it turned out to be a good thing. I swung back around to get Sassy an hour later, and then we headed up to Santa Barbara until everything blew over down here. It was an epic day up there."

"Oh yeah!" Sharky exclaimed. "I heard that. But I was surfing County Line, which was skunky."

"Sorry to hear that." Marina arrived at her van and reached under the rear bumper to reveal that she'd hidden the key there. Then she unlocked the rear doors and set to work boiling water. "Anyhow, while I was in Santa B, I ended up talking to some locals, and they said that sand has been stolen from two beaches up that way as well."

"Really?" I asked. "When?"

"Both in the last two weeks."

"It's the Dubai people!" Sharky exclaimed. "I know it!"

Marina shifted her gaze to me, wondering what this was all about.

I rolled my eyes, indicating that the less she knew, the better. "What happened?"

"Same as down here," Marina reported. "People who were camping out heard some kind of machinery offshore in the middle of the night, and when they woke up in the morning, a lot of sand was gone."

"Aw man," Sharky groaned. "Which spots did they hit?"

"El Capitán was the first," Marina said, then informed me, "That's about ten miles past Santa Barbara. And then Sandyland, which is by Carpinteria."

Sharky groaned again. "If this keeps up, there's not going to be any beaches left!"

My reaction to what Marina had said was very different. I felt a spike of excitement. "What's Carpinteria? A city?"

"Yeah," Marina replied. "It's this funky little beach town on the way to Santa Barbara."

"How far away is it from here?"

"Like sixty miles or so. It takes at least an hour to get there. Sometimes way more with traffic. Why? Is that important?"

"I think so." I already had my phone out and was doing a quick Google search. It only took a few seconds to find what I needed.

"I have to go!" I announced.

"What?" Marina asked, startled by my abruptness. "Why?"

"I think I know who's behind the sand thefts!" I hurried back toward the Colony, pausing only to turn back and say, "Thanks for your help!"

Marina and Sharky were both staring after me, looking thrown by my sudden departure. But I didn't have time to explain things to them. There was one more thing I needed to see to confirm my suspicions.

I ran back along the beach as fast as I could, leaving the public area and entering the Colony. The tide was high that morning, forcing me onto the section of the beach that technically counted as trespassing. I kept running, even though my side ached, until I finally got to the spot I was looking for.

It was right where the dead whale had been two days before.

Due to the tide, most of the beach was underwater, but the part I needed to see was directly beside the seawall.

Just as I had suspected, the bottom rung of the wooden staircase that led to Jackson Cross's house was resting on the sand.

The day before, it had been a foot higher.

I needed to tell Cass. Only, I didn't have her number. But Doc did. I took out my phone to call him.

Summer had texted me while I was running.

Where are you?

We need to talk.

I considered texting her back—or calling—but it seemed more important to alert Cass right away. So I called Doc instead.

The phone rang six times before he answered it, and when he did, he sounded even grouchier than usual. I had probably woken him up. "This better be important."

"It is! I know who the sand thief is!"

"You do?" Doc instantly sounded wide awake. "Who?"

"Jackson Cross!"

"The actor? How do you know?"

"Well . . . ," I began, but then didn't finish.

Because Jackson Cross was coming down the beach toward me, walking Tinkerbell, his Rottweiler.

In my haste to call Doc, I hadn't even thought to look around for the bad guy.

Jackson was blocking my way back to Binka's house—and it was evident that he had overheard me saying I knew all about him. He no longer looked like the nice and friendly person who had offered to help me pick up trash the day before. Apparently, that had all been an act.

Now his true self was showing through. He was glaring at me menacingly, his hands clenched into fists.

Tinkerbell didn't look very nice either. She snarled at me, revealing her sharp, nasty teeth.

I turned around, thinking I could run back to the surfing beach.

Gabriel, Jackson's muscle-bound security man, was coming down the steps from the pool deck behind me, blocking my escape route. The high sea walls of the beach houses were hemming me in on one side, while the ocean hemmed me in on the other.

I was trapped.

19

THE THIEF

"Get that kid!" Jackson ordered.

"Okay." In Gabriel's deep, gravelly voice, even that single word sounded terrifying. However, the security man was so top heavy due to his muscular build, he had to take his time coming down the wobbly wooden staircase from the pool deck.

I used the extra few seconds this bought me to try to figure out a plan of escape. The strip of sand between the ocean and the seawalls of the mansions was only six feet wide, filled with bits of garbage that had washed up and a few remnants of the dead whale that even the seagulls had felt were too nauseating to eat. Ahead of me, toward Binka's house, Jackson stood right in the center of the sandy strip, Tinkerbell at his side. I like dogs a lot, but this one gave me the shivers. If Jackson told her to attack, she could have easily overpowered me.

The seawalls were all too steep to climb. And while each had a staircase leading up to the pool deck, all of them had locked gates at the top. I considered fleeing through the surf, but the water quickly got deep, and big waves were breaking close to shore. It would be difficult—and possibly dangerous—to run through the water, but still, it seemed to be the only option. . . .

Until I realized I had one other possibility of escape. I didn't know if it would work, but I decided to give it a shot.

Gabriel reached the bottom of the staircase and lumbered toward me. "Don't make any trouble," he warned me. "I don't want to hurt you."

"Good," I told him. "Because I don't want to be hurt. So why don't you just let me go, and we'll both get what we want?"

"Sorry," Gabriel said. "Boss's orders." He was only a few feet away from me.

I turned and ran, heading toward Binka's house. My sudden movement caught Gabriel by surprise. It took him a moment to come after me, and, as I had suspected, as a big man, he wasn't built for speed. I actually had to slow down to make sure he stayed close behind me.

Ahead, Jackson went into a defensive crouch, ready to grab

me if I tried to run past him. But that wasn't my plan at all.

Instead, I cut toward the seawall of Jackson's house. Along the base of it lay the four-foot-long section of whale intestine that I had noticed the day before. It was the biggest piece of the whale still remaining on the beach, probably because it was also the most disgusting. No seagull had wanted to eat it, and no human had dared get close enough to remove it. Since a whale's digestive tract is in constant operation, the intestine certainly still had some partially digested food in it—or worse, what remained *after* digestion—and it had been cooking in the sun for the past two days. So the intestine was now bloated with putrid gasses as well, looking somewhat like an enormous, swollen blister on the beach.

Gabriel was so focused on me, he didn't notice the giant entrails until it was too late.

I approached the intestine from one end, with Gabriel right behind me. Just as he was about to lash out, I leaped forward, landing with both feet directly on the central bubble of the distended bowel. The result was like stomping on a very large and rancid whoopee cushion. Everything inside it was suddenly forced out the opening at the end, which Gabriel happened to be standing directly in front of. He was immediately splattered from head to toe by a burst of bile and decomposed krill. Despite his size and imposing demeanor, he reacted to this the way any normal person would have: he freaked out. He stopped pursuing me and shrieked, clawing at his face, trying to wipe the noxious gunk off.

Now that Gabriel was temporarily incapacitated, my plan was to double back past him and flee toward the surfer's beach. Unfortunately, the rotten intestine turned out to be as slippery as an ice rink. My feet skidded out from under me, and I fell on my butt atop it, which resulted in me firing another blast of toxic sludge at Gabriel.

Jackson raced down the beach toward us. Tinkerbell bounded along beside him. Jackson pointed my way and yelled, "Sic him!"

Tinkerbell gave a series of terrifyingly ominous barks and charged, drool dripping from her gums.

I scrambled back to my feet but fought every instinct to run. Tinkerbell was faster than me and would have easily taken me down from behind. Instead, I grabbed a hunk of gooey innards and flung it at the dog, hoping to hit her in the face and produce the same disgusted reaction that Gabriel had displayed.

However, I missed the dog entirely. The glob of whale sailed past her and plopped onto the beach.

I cringed and steeled myself, preparing to be attacked.

Instead, Tinkerbell made an abrupt U-turn in the sand and ran back for the piece of whale I had thrown. She barked once more, in what I now recognized was enthusiasm, her stubby tail wagging happily.

"No!" Jackson shouted at her. "Don't fetch, you idiot! Attack!"

However, it turned out that Tinkerbell had only *looked* menacing. Her charge at me had been playful, rather than aggressive, and now, to Jackson's dismay, she snatched the piece of whale off the beach and carried it to him, eager to play fetch with it.

"Keep that away from me!" Jackson yelled, cringing in revulsion. He tried to scramble past his dog, but she was a living roadblock in his path, desperately wanting him to throw what she had retrieved.

This gave me a chance to escape. I darted back past Gabriel. Unfortunately, by this point, he had managed to clear the half-digested krill from his eyes and was now seething with anger. He lunged for me, forcing me to take evasive action. I veered into the surf just as a wave came in. It caught me in the knees and knocked me off balance, although I still might have recovered had a strand of kelp not lashed itself around one of my legs.

The coast of Southern California is home to many underwater forests of giant kelp, which is the world's largest species of marine algae. The strands are rooted to the seafloor by structures known as holdfasts and are held upright by air sacs on their stalks. Giant kelp is among the fastest-growing organisms on earth, capable of growing two feet in a single day, ultimately reaching lengths of 175 feet. The forests are home to hundreds of marine species, notably sea otters, which are known to wrap themselves in the strands to keep from floating away while sleeping. When the holdfast tears loose—or when a sea urchin eats through the stalk—the kelp drifts away. Some of it washes up on the beaches, in great tangles, and I'd had the misfortune to get snagged in a particularly tenacious strand of it.

I attempted to shake the kelp off my leg but found I'd caught my foot in a loop of it, like a rabbit in a snare. So then I tried to run, dragging the kelp behind me, as though I had the world's biggest piece of toilet paper stuck to the bottom of my shoe.

Gabriel snatched up the distant end of it and pulled, yanking my legs out from under me. I belly flopped into the shallow surf, getting a nose full of seawater. Then, to my horror, Gabriel began reeling me in like a fish, pulling the kelp hand over hand, dragging me along the beach. I tried to kick free to no avail.

Meanwhile, Jackson finally managed to get past Tinkerbell, who stubbornly chased after him with the hunk of whale.

Gabriel had almost pulled me back to him when someone shouted, "Leave him alone!"

It was Sharky. And he hadn't come alone. Behind him stood Marina and a group of other surfers, many of whom were in top physical shape. No one was as big as Gabriel, but altogether, they were an imposing bunch.

At the exact same time, Doc came running down the beach from the other direction. He looked worried, and I suddenly realized that I had stopped talking to him in the middle of my phone call. "Teddy, are you all right?" he yelled to me. "Did anyone hurt you?"

"This guy was about to," I told him, nodding toward Gabriel. I got back to my feet in the shallow surf, soaking wet, caked with sand and draped with kelp.

Gabriel shrank back from everyone, not nearly as tough now that there were lots of adults around to look out for me. "I was only trying to chase the kid off," he claimed. "He was trespassing on Mr. Cross's property. And he slimed me with whale goo!"

"I wasn't doing anything wrong!" I shouted, then pointed at Jackson. "He's the real criminal here! He's the one who's been stealing all the sand from the beaches!"

The surfers all shifted their attention to Jackson and glared at him accusingly.

"That's not true!" Jackson insisted. "That child is a liar and a menace!"

Marina ignored him and asked me, "What's your proof?"

I said, "Yesterday morning I found a cup buried in the sand here. It was from a restaurant called the Spot in Carpinteria. . . ."

"Ooh! I love that place!" Sharky exclaimed. "The milk-shakes are amazing!" Several of the surfers seconded this.

"Big deal, you found some garbage," Jackson snapped. "There's garbage all over the beach. That doesn't prove anything."

"The cup was relatively new, but it was buried several feet under the sand," I said. "The only reason I found it was that the Coast Guard left a trench when they dragged the dead whale away. How would a new cup get buried so deep in the sand so far from Carpinteria?"

"It could have floated down here," Jackson insisted.

"Carpinteria's at least sixty miles away," Doc said. "There's no way a new cup could float that far and end up buried so deep so fast."

Tinkerbell gave up on trying to get Jackson to play fetch and brought the chunk of whale to Doc. Doc gamely tossed it down the beach for Tinkerbell, who happily ran after it, barking enthusiastically.

"A bunch of sand was stolen in Carpinteria just the other day," Marina reported, and several of the surfers chimed agreement.

I looked at Jackson. "The cup I found was probably dropped on the beach up there, sucked up by the boat you used to steal the sand, then spit back out and buried here when the sand was deposited."

"That's all your evidence? A cup?" Jackson asked mockingly. He strode through the surf to confront me. "Where is this magical cup, anyhow?"

"You tricked me into letting you throw it away," I said. "You saw me with it and then came out with a garbage bag and pretended like you clean the beach every day."

Jackson acted as though I had offended his honor. "That wasn't pretending! I *do* clean the beach every day."

"Really?" I asked skeptically. "If you're so concerned about the beaches, then why didn't you come with me to the beach by the lagoon after telling me that's where most of the trash is?" I looked to the surfers. "Have any of you ever seen this guy cleaning the beach?"

The answer was a resounding no.

Sharky glared at Jackson. "The only thing I've ever seen you do is tell me to get off your property! Even though the beach is public land! You're a bad person—and a bad actor! I hated your TV show!"

Jackson was obviously bothered by this, but he did his best to let it slide and gave me a smug look. "Without that cup, it doesn't sound like you have any evidence at all."

"Oh, I've got more." I turned back to the surfers to lay out my case. "Look at the stairs coming down from everyone's homes! The sand has eroded away from the bases of all of them—except Jackson's! It doesn't make any sense that the sand in front of his house would still be high while everyone else's is low—unless he was replacing it!"

The surfers all recognized that I was right. A chorus of agreement went through the crowd.

Even Gabriel seemed surprised. "Hey," he said thoughtfully. "That's true."

"There was a boat anchored right offshore here last night," I went on. "I thought it was a fishing boat, but I realize now it must have been pumping sand. Yesterday, Jackson's steps were a foot above the beach. Today, they go right down to it."

"So the sand shifted," Jackson said dismissively. "That happens all the time around here. It doesn't mean anything."

"Yes it does," Gabriel said, with a surprising amount of anger in his voice. He wheeled on Jackson, whose confidence drained out of him like water from a bathtub.

"What are you doing?" Jackson asked him worriedly. "You're supposed to be dealing with the kid!"

"There's no way that much sand would pile up at your house naturally but not your neighbors' homes," Gabriel said heatedly. "Do you know what kind of ecological damage the theft of sand creates? Do you know about the grunion?"

"Er . . . what?" Jackson asked, slowly backing away from Gabriel.

"They're fish." Gabriel advanced toward Jackson. "But on nights when there's a full moon, they come up on the beaches to lay their eggs in the sand. It's amazing. Thousands of them swim in with each wave. However, if some idiot strips all the sand away, then all those eggs are destroyed, which puts the grunion at threat of extinction. I *like* the grunion. Part of the reason I took the job here is so that I can see them. I don't want them to go extinct. And I don't appreciate that you're endangering them just so you don't have to jump down a foot from your stairs to the beach!"

Jackson was now backed up against his own seawall, very close to the rancid section of intestine, while Gabriel loomed over him. "I didn't do it! I swear!" he mewled.

"Lie to me again and I'll shove your head right up that intestine," Gabriel threatened. "I'll wrap you in it like a burrito."

"Okay!" Jackson screamed. "I did it! But not just because of the drop to the beach! It was for a much more important reason: my property value!"

Jackson actually seemed to think this answer would pacify Gabriel, but instead it only made him angrier. The surfers were equally upset and now crowded around Jackson as well.

Doc was watching everything with an amused smile while Tinkerbell pranced around him.

"Property values?" Marina asked Jackson. "Who cares about your stupid property values?"

"*I* do!" Jackson wailed. "I haven't had a hit movie in a decade. My career is in the toilet. The only asset I have is this house, which I paid way too much for. I need to sell it, but no one wants to pay full value for a place on the beach if there's no beach! So yes, I stole some sand to make it look better—but I wasn't going to do it anymore. And then that dumb whale ended up dead on my property and when the Coast Guard took it, all the sand that I'd brought in got dragged away! So I had to get more. But now I'm done, I swear! I'm putting my house on the market this week, and once I sell, I'm not going to do any more damage to the bunions!"

"Grunion!" Gabriel roared. "How could you live here all these years and not even know about them? Do you ever think about anything in the world besides yourself?"

"Er . . . no," Jackson replied.

"It's not just the grunion you're hurting!" Gabriel snarled. "It's the entire coastal ecosystem!"

"I—I'm really sorry," Jackson stammered, then thought to add, "Please don't hurt me."

"Well you certainly deserve some kind of punishment," Gabriel said. "You ought to go to jail."

I turned to Doc. "That's why I was calling you this morning. So you could contact Cass."

Doc grinned, apparently pleased to have yet another excuse to call her. "I can certainly do that. Although . . . it'd

20

THE ACCOMPLICE

Everyone gathered around me on the beach to hear how I'd figured out the rest of the crime.

"I'm staying in a house that Roswell Crowe used to live in," I explained. "But he lost it to his wife, Binka; they're in the process of getting a divorce. All his contracts and blueprints are still there. Roswell built Jackson's house, which is how they know each other. He dredged out a basement for him—and lots of other people in the Colony. And he has plans to dredge a huge underground parking garage on the beach for a project called Surfside as well. Which means Roswell already owned the equipment to remove all the sand. So when Jackson needed it done, that's who he called."

"But why would Roswell do that for him?" Doc asked.

"Roswell doesn't need the money. Why commit so blatant a crime?"

"To get even with Binka," I explained. "She told me that four weeks ago, the sand in front of her house had suddenly eroded so badly that she had to tape a ladder to her stairs to get down to the beach. Binka thought it was a natural process, but it was much worse at her home than anyone else's. Even though all the houses at the Colony are right next to one another. This happened at the beginning of the sand thefts. Because of their ugly divorce, I'm assuming Roswell was happy to do something nasty to her beach house while making some money on the side." I looked to Jackson. "Am I right so far?"

"Not quite," Jackson answered, now eager to try to make someone else look bad besides himself. "I didn't approach Roswell at all. This was *his* idea! All I did was ask him if he knew how I could build the beach up in front of my house, and he said *he* could do it. He'd already invested in some major dredging equipment for that Surfside project, but it never got built. The environmentalists blocked construction because it was going to destroy the beach, and Roswell got stuck with all the machinery. He was *desperate* to use it. He cut me a great deal, so I agreed. I had no idea he was going to steal the sand from Binka. I thought he was going to get it somewhere legit! He coerced me into all this!"

Doc looked to me. "Think that's accurate?"

"I suppose," I said.

"I think Jackson's telling the truth," Marina put in. "I've seen his movies. He's not that good an actor."

"She's right!" Jackson agreed excitedly. "I'm not!" The moment the words were out of his mouth, he seemed to regret them, but it was too late.

Marina asked me, "But after Roswell had stolen the sand from Binka, why did he continue stealing sand from all those other places?"

"Because you can't just pump sand onto a beach and expect it to stay there," Sharky said, speaking with surprising authority. "If it was eroding away from here before, then it's gonna keep eroding away. Men can't control the world as much as we like to think. Beaches all through Malibu are disappearing. Maybe because we've messed up all the currents through building projects—or maybe because of global warming. Or maybe it's just the natural ebb and flow of the planet. Whatever the case, you can't fight Mother Nature. She'll always win."

Several of the surfers nodded agreement, impressed by this wisdom.

"That's deep," Gabriel said approvingly, then returned his attention to Jackson. "So all your sand washed away, and you couldn't just accept it? You wanted more?"

"Roswell obviously didn't know what he was doing," Jackson said defensively. "He told me we'd only have to do this once, but yes, the sand washed away. So I needed more. Only, Roswell didn't feel he could steal from Binka again, because he was worried she'd catch on, so he took it from down by the lagoon."

"I knew it!" Sharky exclaimed.

"Wait." Doc gave Jackson a curious look. "Roswell just went along with this? Why would he keep stealing sand for you?"

"Er . . . ," Jackson said, looking uneasy about answering.

"You blackmailed him, didn't you?" I asked. "If Binka found out that he'd stolen the sand from her beach, that would have caused problems with the divorce, wouldn't it?"

"Darn straight it would have," Marina agreed. "Binka doesn't own that beach. It's state land. So stealing it was a crime against the government, which wouldn't go over so well in a divorce proceeding."

"All the sand from the state beaches was public property too!" Sharky added, glaring at Jackson. "You stole from the people just to make your home look better!"

Jackson held up his hands to signal his innocence. "I didn't know where Roswell was getting the sand. I just asked him to get it for me."

"Asked?" Gabriel repeated skeptically.

"Okay, maybe I blackmailed him a little. But I really didn't know where it was coming from."

"Sure you didn't," Marina challenged.

I said, "Whatever the case, I'm guessing that Roswell stole from different beaches so that no one would notice the thefts were all connected. He just didn't realize that all the surfers would put it together."

"*You* put it together," Marina corrected. "If it wasn't for you, this jerk would have gotten away with it."

"That's right." Gabriel clapped a meaty hand on Jackson's arm. "So what should we do to make sure he doesn't run off before the feds can get here?"

"I say we duct-tape him to the staircase," Sharky suggested, provoking a chorus of cheers.

"No!" Jackson wailed. "I can't go to jail! It'd be terrible for my public image! There must be a deal we can make. I know a lot of you live in scummy old vans. Maybe you'd like some beds to sleep in for a while? And hot showers? And warm food?"

"We're not taking anything from you," Marina said, then told Gabriel, "Go get some tape."

The surfers all crowded around Jackson.

I suddenly realized I was shivering.

I was soaked and it was chilly outside. I had been so distracted with Jackson that I hadn't noticed how cold my body was.

Doc realized as well. He took off his sweatshirt and wrapped it around me. "Let's get you back to Binka's. Fast. You need a hot shower right away."

"But Jackson . . . ," I began, though I didn't get any further, because my teeth started chattering.

"Trust me, he's not going anywhere. I'll call Cass right now. Go." Doc pointed toward Binka's house.

I started running.

"Thanks, kid!" Sharky yelled after me. And then Marina and the others yelled their thanks as well.

I waved good-bye and raced down the beach. Getting my blood pumping warmed me up a little bit, but I still felt like a human popsicle by the time I reached Binka's house.

Binka had a heated cabinet on her deck so that her pool towels were always warm and toasty. I felt this was a terrible waste of energy—but I grabbed a towel out of it anyhow and had to admit that wrapping it around myself was a wonderful sensation.

Then I used the outdoor shower. I had spent most of the first ten years of my life showering outside at our tent camp; that had involved a solar-heated five-gallon bag of water hung from a tree branch. Binka's shower was much different: it had a smoked-glass door, and the walls and floor were expensively tiled. There was plenty of hot water and a large array of fancy shampoos and soaps. I got into it with my clothes on, since I wanted to rinse them out too. The warm water immediately reinvigorated me.

It took three separate shampooings to get all the sand out of my hair and a great deal of scrubbing to dislodge it from everywhere else on my body. Quite a lot of time had gone by before I finally felt like myself again. I emerged from the shower, swaddled in the towel, to find Doc just returning to the house and wrapping up a phone call. From the rare smile on his face, I could tell he'd been talking to Cass.

"What's going on?" I asked.

"Cass was very pleased to hear you figured out who's been stealing the sand. She's notifying the proper authorities."

"That's great!"

"It is, Teddy. Nice work."

I was pleased to have solved the crime—and received rare praise from Doc—but I still didn't feel terrific. After all, there was still another mystery that I had zero leads on. Although something had occurred to me while I was in the shower. "Doc, do you think there's any way the dead whale could be connected to the stolen sand? Like, would it have beached itself there because of the sand for some reason?"

Doc considered that thoughtfully before answering. "I suppose it's possible. We honestly don't know why whales beach themselves, but there's a lot of speculation that human interference with their environment is to blame. One theory is that all those giant propellers on cargo and cruise ships make so much noise—which carries for hundreds of miles through the water—that they mess up whales' internal navigation systems. But there are plenty of other theories as well. So sure, maybe there was something about the sand from Carpinteria suddenly being moved sixty miles to this beach that confused the whale. But then again, if it was already dying from a bad injury or dehydration or an illness from exposure to some toxins that had been dumped in the ocean, any of that could have led it to beach itself as well."

I sighed, saddened by the thought of the dead whale. "I wish I could figure out who was behind this."

"Go easy on yourself. You've already solved one mystery today. Don't you have a movie premiere soon?"

I checked my watch and gasped. It was much later than I had realized. Since *Final Glory 4* was targeted at families, the premiere was early in the day so that kids could attend. I had gotten so wrapped up with finding the sand thief that I had forgotten all about it. "Oh yeah. Thanks."

I left my soggy clothes hanging in the outdoor shower and hurried back upstairs, wrapped in the towel. I was about to enter my bedroom when Summer exited hers.

The premiere wasn't formal, but Summer was still wearing a nice new outfit. She had also done her hair and makeup.

Summer usually dressed far more casually, so it had been a long time since I had seen her like this. I froze, struck by how beautiful she was. All I could say was "Wow."

Meanwhile, Summer was upset to see that I was only in a towel. "Why aren't you dressed yet? We have to leave in two minutes!"

"I'll get ready fast. I just showered."

"Where?" There was an edge to Summer's voice, as though she was upset at me for something else besides being behind schedule. "Don't you have a shower in your room?"

"Yes, but I used the outdoor one."

"Why? Where have you been? Were you swimming?"

"No. I cracked the sand-theft case! Jackson Cross was the thief! And guess who he was working with?"

I had thought that this news would excite Summer, but to my surprise, it only upset her more. "You went and investigated without me?"

"Er . . . yes."

"Teddy! I told you last night that I wanted to be a part of that!"

"I know, but you were asleep when I went out this morning."

"Are you sure? Did you check?"

"No, but—"

"And then I texted you but you ignored me."

"I didn't! I just didn't notice. Jackson and his body-guard came after me. I nearly ended up in a lot of trouble."

"Which is exactly why you shouldn't be doing any of this on your own! And yet, you totally cut me out! Why? Were you still angry about last night?"

The answer to that was yes. Only I didn't want to admit it. So instead, I got defensive. "No! I was just trying to let you sleep!"

"You could have waited for me. Or woken me up. But instead you went off on your own, like I'm not even a part of this team."

"You didn't seem so excited to be a part of it yesterday!" I knew this was the wrong thing to say, but I couldn't help myself. I was upset that Summer's reaction to learning I'd been in danger had been to get more upset at *me*. And I was still smarting from everything that had happened the day before.

"I went to a concert!" Summer snapped. "By my favorite band! I'm allowed to do something that isn't part of a criminal investigation now and then! But that doesn't mean I don't care about it. Just like if I kiss someone on the cheek, it doesn't mean I don't care about you."

"Then why don't you want to tell everyone that I'm your boyfriend?" I demanded, feeling hurt and irritated all at once.

Summer gave an exasperated sigh. "I don't want to start this again. We have a premiere to go to, and you're not even dressed yet. It *is* okay for me to go to a premiere, right? You're not going to be upset at me for that, too?"

"That depends. Are you going to acknowledge me at all? Or are you going to pretend like I don't exist again?"

Anger flared in Summer's eyes. She looked like she wanted to say something, but then she just turned away and stormed downstairs.

I went into my bedroom and slammed the door behind me.

I knew I had said many of the wrong things in anger. But it seemed to me that Summer had said plenty of wrong things herself. Now we'd had our second fight in less than twelve hours. Suddenly, it seemed like we couldn't talk about anything without it turning into an argument.

Summer hadn't even seemed to care that I'd solved the crime of the sand thefts. And I'd never had the chance to tell her that Binka's husband was also involved.

I had solved a crime and was going to a movie premiere. This should have been a great day all around.

And yet, nothing seemed great about it at all.

21

THE PREMIERE

Summer might not have been interested in who had stolen the sand, but Binka was thrilled to learn that her soon to be ex-husband was a criminal. Since they were still in the midst of a nasty divorce and fighting over every single thing they owned, anything that made Roswell Crowe look bad was very good for Binka. And as Marina had pointed out, stealing sand from public beaches was a federal crime, which was very bad indeed.

Binka and Kandace had a wonderful time on the way to the premiere. They had arranged for a limousine to take us there and spent most of the ride toasting each other with champagne. Both were dressed to impress in stunning outfits from Binka's closet. According to Binka, her shoes alone cost more money than a weeklong all-expenses vacation at FunJungle.

I had never been in a limousine before but had always imagined it would be a lot of fun. I didn't enjoy it at all, though.

Binka kept tousling my hair and calling me "her hero," which normally might have made me feel good, but since I had overheard her saying unkind things about me the night before, everything nice that she said now rang false and made me angry.

Although Summer was the bigger issue. We didn't speak the entire time. We were both irritated at each other, and I felt miserable about it, but there was no privacy in the limo, and I was embarrassed to bring everything back up again in front of Kandace and Binka—and worried that if I did, it might devolve into another fight. So we both just stared awkwardly out the window as the car whisked us down the beach in Malibu and then along the highways in Los Angeles until we finally arrived in Hollywood.

Things did not improve after that.

I had always heard Hollywood was extremely glamorous, but it looked pretty much like any other city I had ever been in. The famous Hollywood Walk of Fame with the stars embedded in the sidewalk turned out to be lined with tacky souvenir shops and run-down businesses. The Hollywood sign was smaller than I had expected; I had also learned it was merely a remnant of an advertisement for real estate, which made it seem far less interesting.

The premiere itself was glitzier. The street in front of the movie theater was closed to traffic for the event. There was an actual red carpet for guests to walk down, and beyond that, a large fake jungle had been created with hundreds of potted trees for the party that would follow the screening. Dozens of police officers patrolled the perimeter to keep out people who weren't invited.

Our limousine was directed to a special drop-off area for premiere guests. The moment we got out, Trish raced up, thrilled to see Binka, Kandace, and—most of all—Summer. She was also dressed to impress, flashing plenty of jewelry and tottering on five-inch heels. "You look fabulous!" she exclaimed. "The paparazzi are going to go wild when they see you! The carpet's this way!" She shunted the three of them toward a staging area manned by lots of security personnel.

I started to follow, but Trish caught my arm. "Not you," she said. "You and I have to stay with the other dregs of humanity." I knew she meant it in a joking way, but it still hurt.

It turned out there was a whole other route to the theater for us. Summer, Binka, Kandace, and the various actors, models, influencers, and other famous people took the red carpet, passing a grandstand full of screaming fans and a gauntlet of photographers and reporters, who implored them to stop and pose for the camera and then peppered them with questions.

Meanwhile, Trish and I joined a much larger group of nonfamous people, most of whom, Trish explained, had worked on the movie in some way or another. They were camera operators, caterers, electricians, secretaries at the studio, or any of a hundred other jobs. Many had their children with them. Our route led directly beneath the grandstand to a side entrance for the movie theater. While the red carpet had dozens of spotlights facing it, even though it was the middle of the day, our path was dark and dingy and strewn with garbage that had been dropped through the stands.

"I know this makes it seem like we're second-class citizens," Trish told me, "but even the most powerful studio executives have to come this way." She then pointed out a few of them, as if that would make me feel better.

It didn't. As we passed under the stands, I heard dozens of fans screaming Summer's name, as well as a few of the reporters' questions:

"What's it like dating Wynn Gyoko?"

"Is it serious between you two?"

"Is he a good kisser?"

I couldn't hear Summer's answers. She was too far away and the crowd was too loud.

As we reached the end of the stands, I caught a glimpse of the red carpet. Summer, Kandace, and Binka were all posing before the horde of paparazzi, although most of the lenses appeared to be aimed at Summer.

"She's a natural, isn't she?" Trish asked.

I had to admit that, despite how much Summer claimed to hate talking to reporters, she appeared to be very at ease in front of them.

We had only paused for a few seconds before a security guard barked at us. "No loitering! Get to your seats!"

"Relax, we're going," Trish told him, then hooked a hand through my arm and led me inside.

The theater was the largest I had ever seen, with a massive screen and thousands of seats. Everyone was milling about in the aisles and the lobby, chatting with one another and gobbling free popcorn. Away from the fans and the paparazzi, all the actors and other celebrities were behaving like normal people, talking to friends and shepherding their children. Even Brock Stoneman, the star of the franchise, looked like a regular human being.

Trish steered me to our seats, then said, "I have to go say hi to some people," and hurried away, leaving me all alone.

Since I didn't know anyone but Summer, Kandace, and Binka, I didn't have anyone to talk to. So I simply sat in my seat, alone, and hoped that they would arrive soon.

I hadn't been there long before I received a text from Doc:

Bad news. Cass says no dice on investigating any of the ships.

I groaned in frustration, then texted back: Why not?

Too expensive. Too time-consuming. No $$$ or man-power.

Don't they want to find out who killed the whale?

Of course. But they have limited resources and lots of battles to fight. Sorry.

That was all I got out of him, which made my sour mood even worse.

It was another twenty minutes before Summer, Kandace, and Binka finally showed up. The theater staff had already made several announcements that the movie needed to start and pleaded for everyone to get to their seats. The head of the studio was thanking everyone for coming by the time Summer and the others squeezed into our row. They were still getting situated when the lights dimmed, the audience cheered, and the movie began.

I was frustrated with how things had gone that day and annoyed that I had been left on my own for so long. I had hoped that the movie would lift my spirits, but it didn't. Because the movie was terrible.

The first *Final Glory* hadn't exactly been a cinematic

masterpiece, but it had at least been fun. *Final Glory 4* was as absurd as its own title and the filmmakers got practically every single thing about the Amazon wrong. The heroes tumbled over thousand-foot waterfalls that don't exist on that river and miraculously survived without so much as a scratch. Then they battled sharks and grizzly bears, neither of which live in the Amazon basin, along with an anaconda of biologically impossible proportions. The final action sequence took place inside the ruins of a lost civilization that looked like it had been built by ancient Greeks, who hadn't even known that the Amazon existed. I'm well aware that some movies aren't supposed to be taken seriously, but it drives me nuts when they get basic facts of science wrong.

On top of that, the movie simply wasn't interesting. It felt like a movie I had seen many times before. At some point, I stopped paying attention and found myself thinking about the exploding whale.

Without the government's help, it seemed increasingly likely that the crime would go unsolved. I considered asking J.J. McCracken to fund the investigation, or approaching an environmental group like Sea Shepherd, which was known for going to great lengths to protect whales, but I had a feeling that neither of those options would go anywhere. The list of potential suspects was too big, too powerful, too international, and almost impossible to pursue.

Which was infuriating, because someone had obviously tried to cover up a crime. Why else would they blow up the whale before it could be autopsied? They had concealed evidence—and were now literally going to get away with murder.

Then I found myself returning to the idea that perhaps blowing up the whale hadn't been about hiding evidence at all.

Maybe one of Jackson Cross's neighbors had found out he was stealing sand from them and decided to get even by blowing up the carcass to cover his home with whale guts— only they'd put in too much explosive and splattered all the nearby homes as well. Or maybe they had an entirely different reason for hating Jackson; I had seen firsthand what a jerk he could be.

Or maybe the detonation was intended to hit one of the other houses on the beach. Or a bunch of them. Marina and Sharky had both seemed resentful of the billionaires that lived in the Colony. There were probably other surfers who felt the same way. Had one of them decided to blow up the whale in order to cause property damage—or perhaps merely as a prank on the rich folks?

Or was the idea simply to frame Chase Buckingham

or Scooter Derman? Maybe those guys had enemies; now Chase was in jail, Scooter had fled the country, and whoever had blown up the whale was free and clear. It was a bizarre crime to frame someone for—and yet, it had worked.

With this angle, there were suddenly dozens of new potential criminals, if not hundreds: residents of the Colony, surfers, anyone whom Chase or Scooter might have rubbed the wrong way. It was all overwhelming.

By the time the end credits for the movie rolled and the audience burst into applause, I was in an extremely crummy mood. But while the movie was over, the festivities were just beginning.

We all funneled back out of the theater for the party in the fake jungle. Even though all the plants were potted, they had been artfully arranged to shield most of the buildings around us, giving the impression that we were really in a tropical forest rather than smack in the middle of one of the largest cities on the planet. At our feet, the asphalt of the street had been covered with acres of fake turf, and all of the catering staff wore safari clothing. In the center of it all were dozens of tables piled with food—and, as Trish had promised, there were plenty of animals as well.

The animals were owned by people who rented them out for use in the movies. In fact, many of the animals at the party had appeared in the movie as well. I noticed that precautions had been taken to ensure their safety; each animal had a crew of trainers to care for it and make sure that no party guests did anything dangerous or foolish nearby. But still, it saddened me to see the animals in such strange surroundings, basically being used as props for party photos.

Except for a pair of scarlet macaws, a sloth, and a few llamas, none of the animals were even from South America. There were two Asian elephants, a pair of lion cubs, a chimpanzee, an orangutan, a leopard, a zebra, a black bear, a wolf, a pelican, a bald eagle, a raven, and an assortment of monkeys and lemurs. Although there are monkeys in the Amazon, every single one at the party was from the wrong continent.

However, I was still intrigued by the menagerie. Summer, Kandace, and Binka were all being mobbed by fans, leaving me by myself again, so I wandered over to see the animals.

Most already had long lines of people waiting to take pictures with them. The only exception was the raven, which was common enough that no one seemed to care about it. An older woman with a long braid of silver hair was holding it, seeming perfectly happy to not have to deal with the crowds. And yet, she smiled as I approached.

"Ah," she said. "Here's a young man who knows a thing or two about animals."

"Why do you say that?"

"Because you recognize that my friend Poe here is just as fascinating as all these other creatures. And possibly smarter than the whole lot put together, with the exception of the chimp."

"I think the elephants might not appreciate hearing you say that."

The woman laughed. "You *do* know your animals. I'm Shasta, the head trainer for Animal Encounters."

"Teddy," I said. "Does anyone in this city know which animals are actually from South America?"

"Well, I do, of course. The problem is, South American animals aren't exciting enough for the movie folks. The largest animal down there is the tapir—and, let's face it, a tapir's just not as thrilling as an elephant."

"There's jaguars."

"True. But put a jaguar next to a lion or a tiger and it looks kind of puny. The movie execs don't want puny. Want to hold Poe?"

"Yes! Is that all right?"

"Sure. This guy's harmless. And he's exceptionally well behaved, unlike some other animals I could mention."

"Which ones?"

Shasta leaned close and whispered, as though it was a secret. "The lemurs. They might be more closely related to us than Poe, but they're a bunch of idiots compared to him. You can't even teach them to control their urine. Spook one just a tiny bit and it'll pee like a firehose."

"So . . . no letting the guests hold them then?"

"Nope. As much as I'd love to see one soil the CEO of the studio, nobody's allowed to touch any of the animals except this one. Hold your arm out."

I did. Shasta gave a quick whistle, and Poe hopped from her arm onto mine.

Even though the bird was quite big, he barely weighed more than an extra-large bag of potato chips.

"Good boy," Shasta said.

There was a roar of excitement from nearby. A trainer had got the black bear to stand on its hind legs behind one of the stars of the movie and her children for a photo.

"You think that's impressive?" Shasta muttered, then said, "Poe, go get me a cookie."

The bird leaped off my arm, flapped over to the dessert buffet, snatched a cookie, and flew right back, alighting on my shoulder and depositing the dessert in Shasta's hand.

"He's even smart enough to get chocolate chip instead of oatmeal raisin," Shasta observed. "Of course, all the execs were mighty disappointed that I wouldn't let guests touch the other animals. They all thought it'd be great publicity to have photos of the celebrities holding chimps and riding elephants. And this is *after* one of the stars got bitten by a lion cub on the set."

"Oh yeah," I said. "I heard about that."

"Of course you did. Everyone in the universe heard that story. And the media blew it way out of proportion. They said the cub attacked the actor when, really, the actor tried to yank away a steak the cub was eating. So it bit him. Just like any pet dog or cat would have. But who cares if they get their facts straight, right? All they want is the story. So I asked the execs, 'Do you really want to have two thousand people poking and prodding these animals while every news media outlet on earth is covering the event?' You make a mistake once, and everyone might forgive you and say, 'Okay, accidents happen.' But make a mistake *twice* and you've got a PR disaster on your hands."

"Oh wow," I said. Not only because Shasta's advice was smart, but because it had made me realize something important. Something that hadn't occurred to me before.

Shasta frowned suddenly. "Speaking of PR disasters, looks like one's about to happen." She was looking toward the lions, where Brock Stoneman was disobeying the wildlife handlers and picking up one of the cubs for the paparazzi. "Keep an eye on Poe for me. I'll be right back." She darted into the crowd.

I watched her go but wasn't really focused on her. Instead,

I was thinking over the new idea that had come to me. The more I thought about it, the more it made sense. There were still some pieces of information I needed to find. . . .

But if I was right, then maybe I could catch who had killed the whale after all.

THE DEDUCTION

I could have looked up the information I needed on my phone right away, but there was something I wanted to do first.

I searched the party for Summer.

True, things had been prickly between us lately. However, not sharing what I was thinking with her would only make things worse—and the last thing I wanted to do was make things worse. In fact, what I really wanted to do, more than anything else at that moment, was have Summer help figure out the case with me.

I spotted her standing with her mother and Binka, talking to some people in suits. Kandace and Binka looked very excited about the conversation, while Summer appeared bored. She was watching all the animals, and I knew her well enough to realize that she was wishing she was visiting them, rather than talking to a bunch of adults.

I hurried through the crowd toward her. Several people gave me odd looks, although I didn't realize why until I got to Summer.

"Hey," I said.

"Hey," she replied. "Why is there a raven on your shoulder?"

I had forgotten about Poe. He weighed so little, I hadn't even noticed him in all my excitement. Now I'd been running through the party looking like a discount pirate who couldn't afford a parrot. "This is Poe. He's trained. I think I figured out who killed the whale."

Summer immediately seemed to forget about everything else going on around her. Her attention was completely riveted on me. "Who?"

Binka suddenly stepped between us, giving me a look that indicated she wasn't happy to see me at all. "Teddy, you're interrupting a conversation with some very important people." She tried to steer Summer back to the people in suits, but Summer held her ground.

"They're not nearly as important as *this*," she said, then turned her back on Binka to face me. "Tell me everything."

Binka scowled, but behind her back, Kandace grinned and gave me a friendly wink.

I returned my attention to Summer. "I've been trying to figure out who would go through so much trouble to get rid of a dead whale. And I just realized something! While it would look bad for an oil company or a fishing trawler or a cargo ship to kill a whale, you know what would *really* look bad? Killing *two* whales."

Summer nodded, obviously intrigued. "That makes sense. But who . . . ?"

"The other day, you mentioned a ship that had hit a whale on the way to San Francisco. Do you remember what it was called?"

"Yes. The *Golden Lotus*."

"Where's that ship *now?*"

Summer's eyes went wide as she understood what I was thinking. "You think it came this way?"

"I know how to find out." I took out my phone and brought up the ship-tracking site that Doc and I had been using the night before. Summer crowded beside me to watch. She gasped with surprise when she first saw how many ships were on the planet—the same way that I had. Then I felt her tense with excitement as I entered *Golden Lotus* in the search. I was equally on edge, wanting to see if my theory was correct.

The *Golden Lotus* was in Long Beach.

I brought up its recent travel information. It had arrived at the port for repairs five days before.

"That's right before the dead whale washed up on the beach!" Summer exclaimed. "And its route took it past Malibu!"

"The ship had already been in the news for killing the first whale," I deduced. "Then they bring it down here—and it strikes *another* whale on the way. It doesn't end up with the whale stuck on the bow like the first time, but they still hit it. . . ."

"And then a whale shows up dead on the beach nearby," Summer added breathlessly. "They figure it has to be the same whale, and they know an autopsy will prove that it died from a ship strike—or maybe even prove the *Golden Lotus* did it. Like maybe the whale had some paint on its body that matched the color of the ship. Or something like that."

"The shipping company knows that if people find out they've killed a second whale, it's going to be a public relations disaster, so they decide to get rid of the evidence by blowing the whale up."

"It totally makes sense. Teddy, you're a genius!" Summer flashed me a proud smile, but it only lasted a moment. "Only, how do we prove this?"

"Two ways. First, we tell Cass to have a team check out the *Golden Lotus* in Long Beach and see if they can find any evidence of a second whale strike."

"Do you think NOAA can do that?"

"I don't know," I admitted. "But it's only one ship to

inspect and it's not too far away, so maybe that's possible."

"What's the second thing?"

"If the company that owns the *Golden Lotus* blew up the whale to protect their image, then someone in their public relations department must have known about it. Maybe we can find that person."

"How?"

I pointed to a line of information on the tracking app. "The *Golden Lotus* is owned by TransPacific Shipping, which is based in Long Beach. That means they probably use a local public relations agency. Trish said she knows practically everyone in the business here. So maybe she knows at least one person at the company."

Summer frowned. "That seems like a real long shot."

"Maybe, but it couldn't hurt to ask her, right?"

"I guess not." Summer looked around the party, then pointed. "She's right over there! Let's go."

Trish was standing close to Brock Stoneman, who was still posing with the lion cubs. She was talking to another woman, both of them holding glasses full of shrimp cocktail. Summer and I hurried across the party to them.

"Any time you want to ditch the raven, feel free," Summer told me.

"I told the trainer I'd watch him, and now he won't leave me," I explained.

"Classic Teddy," Summer said, although it sounded like a compliment.

We arrived at Trish's side. She brightened immediately upon seeing Summer—although she didn't appear nearly as excited to see that I was tagging along, especially with a raven on my shoulder.

"Summer!" Trish exclaimed. "We were just talking about you!" She indicated the woman she had been talking to. "This is Suzanne Patmore. She's the president of the motion picture company that made the movie. Suzanne, this is Summer McCracken."

"It's a pleasure to meet you," Suzanne said graciously.

"I really liked the movie," Summer said, even though I knew that she hadn't. Since Trish had made no attempt to introduce me, Summer did it. "This is Teddy Fitzroy. He usually doesn't have a raven on his shoulder."

Suzanne laughed. "I can see you've met Poe. I've been stuck with him on set a few times." I had expected that a studio executive would be intimidating, but she seemed as kind and friendly as any of my friends' parents.

"It's nice to meet you," I told her, although I couldn't bring myself to lie about liking the movie.

Trish quickly went into full public relations mode. "Summer is a real up-and-comer in the social media influencer world. She was already a hot commodity because her parents are J.J. and Kandace McCracken, but lately, she has gained plenty of attention for her strong environmental stance. Plus, as you've probably heard, she and Wynn Gyoko from the Village Idiots are dating."

Summer didn't appreciate this last statement at all. "That is not true," she informed Suzanne. "I'm dating Teddy."

I took a step back, surprised that Summer had admitted this in public—but very pleased she had done so.

On the other hand, Trish was obviously thrown by Summer's statement. She seemed baffled that anyone would pick me over the lead singer of the Village Idiots. "But . . . Wynn is so rich. And famous."

"I could give a rat's patoot about someone being rich and famous," Summer replied. "Wynn might be a great singer, but it turns out, he's dumb as a lamppost. While Teddy here is the smartest person I've ever met. In fact, he just figured out who killed that whale in Malibu."

Trish was so stunned by all of this that she gagged on her shrimp cocktail. A large piece of crustacean flew from her mouth.

Poe took off, caught the shrimp in midair, then flapped back to my shoulder and gulped it down.

Meanwhile, Suzanne Patmore seemed very intrigued by Summer's claim. She looked to me, impressed. "You solved that mystery?"

"Teddy has solved *plenty* of mysteries," Summer said proudly. "Like, he's the one who figured out who stole Li Ping the panda earlier this year when even the FBI couldn't do it."

"That was you?" Suzanne asked me, even more interested now. "That's amazing!"

"I didn't do it alone," I said quickly. "Summer helped. We really work as a team."

Summer beamed at me and slipped her hand into mine. "Well, yeah, but like I said, Teddy's really the brains of the operation. I'm more like the Dr. Watson to his Sherlock Holmes."

"That is fascinating," Suzanne said. "A real-life, honest-to-goodness team of kid detectives. So who killed the whale?"

"The *Golden Lotus*," Summer announced. "It's the same cargo ship that killed the whale near San Francisco earlier this summer. Then, on the way here, it hit the second whale and injured it so badly that it died too."

"Oh come now," Trish said. She seemed annoyed that the conversation had shifted to the crime instead of Summer's potential career as an influencer. "That sounds ridiculous."

"Not to *me*," Suzanne said, then called out, "Brock!"

Brock Stoneman was passing by; Shasta had finally convinced him to stop manhandling the lion cubs. He came right over. "Hey, boss," he said to Suzanne.

"I want you to meet some seriously impressive kids," Suzanne told him. "*Real* heroes. This is Teddy and Summer. They figured out who killed that whale in Malibu."

"Do you know who blew it up, too?" Brock asked. "Because it happened right near my beach house. A vertebra the size of a Thanksgiving turkey came through my kitchen window and totaled my breakfast nook."

"The shipping company did that to get rid of the evidence!" Summer declared. "By the way, you were amazing in the movie."

"Thanks," Brock said, looking genuinely flattered. "You didn't think I seemed wooden? The critics said I seemed wooden in the last one, so this time I employed the Stanislavsky technique. I really tried to *be* my character, not just pretend to be him."

"And it really came across," Summer said, which made Brock smile like a kindergartener who had just received a gold star.

Suzanne Patmore held up a finger. "Hold on. The same shipping company that killed the whale also blew it up?"

"Well, that's just a theory so far," I said, still having trouble believing that I was talking to Brock Stoneman, one of the biggest movie stars on earth. "But we were thinking that maybe Trish could help us see if we're right."

"Me?" Trish asked, startled. "What do *I* have to do with all this?"

"You're in public relations," Summer told her. "And Teddy and I were thinking that blowing up the whale was a big PR move by the shipping company trying to protect their image."

"Ooh!" Brock exclaimed. "A corporate cover-up! This would make a great movie!"

"It really could," Suzanne said thoughtfully.

"I'm not so sure," Trish said quickly. "I don't think whales are trending well these days. The public is much more into dolphins."

"Anyhow," Summer went on, "you told us that you know almost everyone in PR in LA, so we thought maybe you would know whoever does it for TransPacific Shipping."

"I might have been exaggerating a bit," Trish said.

"Hardly," Suzanne told her. "You're the most connected person in town. At the very least, you must know someone who knows someone at this company."

"I really can't imagine that's true," Trish insisted.

"What's with the stonewalling?" Brock asked teasingly. "You're not in league with the bad guys here, are you, Trish?" Then he laughed at his own joke.

I didn't find it so funny. For someone whose job it was to connect people, Trish was now doing everything she could to prevent this from happening. Which seemed very odd to me.

Then Suzanne laughed along with Brock. It didn't appear that she really thought he was funny. She was just humoring her biggest star.

Trish joined in, laughing as well. She didn't seem to think Brock was that funny, either. She was only laughing with relief that he wasn't actually accusing her.

Her laugh was really strange. Three short, high-pitched chirps. Like a cartoon mouse with the hiccups.

The *exact same* laugh Scooter Derman had made when imitating the woman who'd conned him into blowing up the whale.

Which confirmed my suspicions about why Trish was acting so strangely.

Summer gasped in surprise when she heard the laugh, putting everything together as well.

She pointed at Trish accusingly and exclaimed, "You're Sadie!"

Trish gagged on another piece of shrimp cocktail, which provoked Poe into launching himself after it once again.

"No," Brock told Summer. "This is Trish."

"I know," Summer said. "But she pretended to be someone named Sadie two nights ago to frame these two dumb college guys for blowing up the whale."

"She made them think it was a harmless prank," I explained. "That it would only be a small explosion. But Trish arranged for a blast big enough to destroy the whole carcass, and then made sure her fall guys were standing nearby with all the evidence that was needed to convict them. Meanwhile, TransPacific Shipping got off free and clear."

Trish gaped at us, obviously caught by surprise at how much of the story we had been able to put together, though she tried to recover. "That is the most ludicrous story I have ever heard. I didn't have a thing to do with that whale."

"Then why are your armpits sweating like it's the Fourth of July?" Summer demanded.

Sure enough, the patches of Trish's dress under her arms were soaked. In addition, her hands were trembling so much that her remaining shrimp jiggled in her cocktail glass. She was obviously extremely nervous.

Even Brock seemed to realize she was guilty. "What happened on that beach was awful," he told her angrily. "My breakfast table was one of a kind! I had it handmade by native craftsmen in Indonesia! It was irreplaceable!"

"Also, the shipping company killed a second whale, destroyed the evidence, and framed two innocent people," Suzanne pointed out.

"Right," Brock agreed. "That was bad too."

"I didn't do anything wrong!" Trish protested, then pointed at Summer and me. "These two kids are making things up. I think maybe *they* blew up the whale, and now they're trying to pin it on me!"

"What?" I asked. "Now *that's* ridiculous."

Thankfully, Suzanne didn't believe it. "Why don't we tell all this to the police and let them decide who's lying?" she asked, then turned to a passing caterer. "There are several police officers working security outside the party," she said. "Go find two and bring them to me."

"And you are?" the caterer asked.

"The person who runs the company that's footing the bill for this entire event."

"I'll be right back, ma'am." The caterer scurried away.

Trish was now looking as skittish and twitchy as a rabbit that had been cornered by a fox. "You can't be serious about this," she said, backing away from us.

"Stop," Brock warned. "You're not going anywhere until we get to the bottom of this." He reached out to grab her arm.

Trish flung her shrimp cocktail into his face and fled.

I had expected that Brock would have had no trouble at all chasing her down. After all, Trish was stick thin, wearing a skintight dress and high heels, while Brock was one of the world's biggest action stars. In the movies, he routinely faced extreme danger and fought multiple bad guys at once. But in real life, he was completely incapacitated by the shrimp cocktail. "It's in my eyes!" he wailed. "It stings!" He stumbled about blindly and bowled over a caterer, who dropped a massive platter of crab legs.

It crashed to the ground, startling a nearby chimpanzee, which screeched in fright and leaped out of its trainer's arms onto a buffet table, catapulting a large bowl of gazpacho into the crowd.

While everyone was distracted by the commotion, Trish was getting away.

Which left only Summer and me to go after her.

THE HOSTAGE

Trish raced through the crowd as fast as she could go, but she was hampered by her fancy shoes and her dress, which was so tight that her legs might as well have been bound together at the knees. As a result, even though she was small of stature, she moved like a bull in a china shop, banging into guests, caterers, and landscaping, leaving a trail of chaos in her wake. Within only a few seconds, she bowled over three studio lawyers, five trays of glassware, and a large potted palm tree, which toppled into the animal encounter area, spooking the zebra and the lion cubs.

Meanwhile, the chimpanzee was running amok in the catering area. It bolted through the South American buffet, sending empanadas and plantains flying, then bounded onto the dessert table, where it toppled a chocolate fountain. Several caterers tried to grab the chimp, but it defended itself with baked goods, pelting them with apple-rhubarb crumble and raspberry cheesecake. Brock Stoneman had just managed to wipe the cocktail sauce from his eyes when he was nailed in the face with a banana cream pie, which promptly blinded him again. He blundered into the seafood station, knocking a pyramid of boiled shrimp to the ground.

Each of these events sparked more disorder, as other animals got spooked or party guests panicked. The macaws squawked and flapped their wings. The pelican broke free and swallowed an entire smoked salmon in one gulp. The zebra bucked and punted a honey-glazed ham across the entire party, where it caromed off the head of one of the top entertainment reporters in the country.

Guests screamed, shrieked, and fled—although most of the kids at the event watched everything wild-eyed, as though all of this had been planned for their entertainment. Only the elephants seemed unfazed. They remained calm and serene, then took advantage of the chaos and started eating the landscaping.

Summer and I chased Trish through all of this, ducking pies, leaping upended tables, skirting panicked guests and escaped wildlife. Somewhere along the line, Poe decided he would be safer airborne and took flight, although he made a quick detour to grab a few more shrimp.

Ahead of us, Trish veered away from the guests and wove through the forest of potted plants that created the fake jungle backdrop for the party. After her impractical shoes made her nearly topple one too many times, she tore them off her feet in frustration and flung them at us. The spiked heels turned out to be formidable weapons; one of them barely missed putting my eye out and embedded in a banana tree, while the other sailed out of the jungle and jabbed the zebra in the rump, provoking another round of wild bucking.

But even without her shoes, Trish's ability to run was still hampered by her party dress. Summer and I were closing in and she knew it. In addition, the entire party was surrounded by a temporary fence. It had been erected to keep fans from sneaking into the event, but now it prevented Trish from escaping as well. She made a brief attempt to climb it, but it was futile; in her tight dress, she couldn't even lift her legs. She screamed in frustration, then cut back through the jungle with Summer and me right behind her.

Trish burst through a curtain of palm fronds and found herself back in the animal encounter area, although nobody was getting their photos taken anymore; instead, everyone was transfixed by the pandemonium that had erupted. A portable wood-fired pizza oven had been knocked over and set some of the potted trees on fire, the llamas were stampeding down the red carpet, the chimpanzee had run out of pies and was now pelting the crowd with profiteroles—and Brock Stoneman, in decidedly nonheroic fashion, was shoving elderly women and young children aside to escape the leopard. Meanwhile, the leopard had no interest in any of the humans at all and was busily devouring a large roast beef it had swiped from the carving station.

None of the security guards who had been hired for the party seemed to have any idea what to do. Most of them were gaping at everything in astonishment. The closest one to us didn't even notice as Trish emerged from the fake jungle behind him.

Trish instantly realized there was no way to escape through all the mayhem. To make matters worse for her, Suzanne Patmore was headed our way, leading two policemen. She pointed at Trish and shouted, "There she is!"

Directly beside Trish, an animal trainer was holding a species of lemur called an indri. Lemurs are members of the primate family, which means they are more closely related to monkeys, apes, and humans than most other animals. An indri is black and white, with enormous, bulging eyes and extremely fuzzy ears that stick straight out from its head; it looks like a Muppet that has just stuck a finger into an electrical socket.

In desperation, Trish grabbed the indri from its trainer, then snatched the security guard's Taser and held it dangerously close to the lemur's neck. "Everyone back off or I'll zap this ugly koala!" she warned.

Summer and I stopped in our tracks at the edge of the fake jungle, only a few feet away from Trish. Suzanne Patmore and the police froze as well.

"Er . . . ," I said. "That's not a koala."

"Of course it is!" Trish snapped.

"You really don't know anything about animals, do you?" Summer asked her.

"I know they're delicious and make great shoes," Trish replied, then pointed the Taser at the indri. "And this one's going to die unless someone finds me a getaway car!"

Summer gasped, as did much of the crowd around us, who had now noticed the hostage drama playing out. The indri looked startled—but then, with their bulbous eyes, indris *always* look startled, so I wasn't sure if it was truly worried or not.

"Why don't you put the lemur down and give yourself up?" Suzanne Patmore asked. "Running won't solve anything. You're only going to make things worse for yourself."

"I didn't do anything wrong!" Trish insisted. "I didn't hit a whale with a ship and kill it! I didn't rig the explosives to blow the whale up! That was all the shipping company!"

"But you *did* set up Chase and Scooter," I reminded her.

"I didn't even want to do that! All I did was suggest that TransPacific find some fall guys to pin the explosion on. I had no idea that they would force *me* to do it. But they didn't want to bring in anyone else. Am I getting that getaway car or not?"

"We're working on it," a policeman informed her.

"Well work faster!" Trish yelled. "This koala smells like bad cheese."

There was a soft rustle of wings above me, and Poe the raven landed on my shoulder once again. He had yet another shrimp clutched in his beak, which he quickly gulped down. He had eaten so much that he seemed to have gotten heavier since I'd last held him.

Trish looked at me skittishly. "What are you doing with that bird?"

"Nothing," I said. "He just landed on me."

"Why?"

"Because he likes me, I guess."

"Well don't try anything funny with it!"

"What can I possibly do with a bird?" I asked, although the moment I said it, I had an idea.

Trish wasn't the only one watching Poe with concern. The indri was too, which made sense, as one of the natural enemies of lemurs are birds of prey. Ravens don't hunt the way that hawks or eagles do, but to a lemur, he still looked like a threat.

On the other side of Trish and the indri, the party was descending even further into madness. The orangutan was gorging on a fruit plate, the wolf had joined the leopard in devouring everything at the carving station, most of the buffet tables had been toppled, and the chimpanzee had finally tired of throwing food and was now wallowing in a giant bowl of pudding. The only desserts left on the table were a smattering of baked goods.

"Poe," I said to the raven, "get me a cookie."

The bird obediently took to the air, flying in the most direct route to the dessert table, which took it directly over Trish and the indri.

The lemur squawked in fright and behaved in exactly the way Shasta had told me it would: it urinated all over Trish.

"My dress!" Trish shrieked, and flung her hostage to the ground.

The security guard who she'd stolen the Taser from immediately tackled her.

The weapon tumbled from her grasp and landed beside the indri.

Trish tried to grab the Taser, screaming in frustration. "This dress cost three thousand dollars! And you ruined it, you stupid koala!" Her fingers grazed the weapon's handle.

Realizing that she meant harm, the indri reflexively grabbed the Taser away from her and accidentally pulled the trigger. The Taser fired at Trish, shocking her so badly that her entire body quivered.

The police rushed the stage. Brock Stoneman was right behind them. Now that he'd realized the leopard meant him no harm, he was playing the hero to the hilt, seemingly unaware that he had banana cream filling caked in his hair. "It's all right!" he announced to the crowd. "You're all safe now!"

A generator promptly exploded, setting even more of the fake jungle on fire.

"Although," Brock added, "it might be smart to head for the exits. I'll lead the way!" He fled through the crowd to escape.

Poe flew back to my shoulder with a chocolate chip cookie and dropped it into my hand.

The police were handcuffing Trish, who was wailing. "I don't want to go to jail! I'll give you incriminating evidence on everyone involved in the whale explosion! Or I know of plenty of other criminals I could rat out!"

Suzanne Patmore came along. She was watching everything with a somewhat shell-shocked expression.

"Sorry about the party," I said.

"Honestly, this will generate far more publicity than

a normal party would have." Suzanne looked down at the indri. "I can't believe Trish just got tased by a lemur."

"*I* can," Summer said. "This sort of thing happens all the time when Teddy's around."

"Really?" Suzanne looked at me curiously. "Your life sounds like it'd make for a great movie. We should talk."

Epilogue

THE POD

"Dolphins off the starboard bow!" Doc shouted.

I looked in the direction he was pointing. Sure enough, a half dozen dorsal fins were slicing through the water, only a hundred yards away from us.

"I see them!" Cass whooped enthusiastically, then turned our speedboat, and we raced across the ocean toward the dolphins.

We had returned to Long Beach three days after the movie premiere to search for whales again, although this time, Cass had convinced NOAA to loan us a bigger, faster, and safer boat. The idea was to spend more time watching the giant creatures, since our last encounter had been rushed (and very frightening). The boat seated ten people and had a cabin below with a kitchenette and—more importantly—a small bathroom. The large motors on the stern had allowed us to range farther from the port, so we were now cruising along the bluffs of the Palos Verdes Peninsula. It was only a few miles from the port, but we were still out of sight of the container ships and the oil rigs. Here, steep cliffs rose directly from the water's edge; at times, with the pristine rocky coast on one side and the ocean on the other, I could almost imagine that we off were in the wilderness, rather than on the fringe of the second largest metropolitan area in the United States.

Since there was plenty of room aboard, Summer and Kandace had come with us. The trip was a reward for our help figuring out who had been behind killing the whale—and then blowing up the carcass. Trish had quickly made good on her offer to turn over evidence against her accomplices in return for less jail time. She had provided dozens of emails and recorded phone calls with executives at TransPacific Shipping, revealing their desperate plot to destroy the evidence that the *Golden Lotus* had been responsible for the death of a second whale.

The emails also provided evidence as to *how* the fatal incident had occurred. It turned out that the captain of the *Golden Lotus* had ignored the official shipping lanes laid out to protect marine wildlife. Instead of staying on the western side of Channel Islands National Park near Malibu, he had traveled to the east of them, following the narrow strait between the islands and the mainland. This had saved a slight bit of time and fuel, but he had passed directly through a marine sanctuary, where the ship had struck the young whale. Once all this information was made public, TransPacific Shipping had immediately accused the captain of violating maritime law, while the captain claimed the company had ordered him to do it to cut down on costs. They were already suing each other.

Meanwhile, those same emails revealed that TransPacific hadn't forced Trish to recruit Chase and Scooter as fall guys. In fact, the plan had been Trish's idea from the start, although TransPacific had hired the demolition experts to blow up the whale. Trish wasn't doing as well financially as it appeared. All the jewelry and expensive dresses she wore to make herself *look* successful—as well as her high-end sports car—had left her in massive debt. She had been desperate to dig herself out, which was how she had ended up freelancing for TransPacific in the first place—and why she had been willing to break the law for them. The company had promised her a large cash payment in return for getting rid of the dead whale. Turning over evidence had helped her case, but Cass felt that, at the very least, Trish was going to end up doing several hundred hours of community service as a penalty for her crime.

"If there's any justice, they'll make her pick every single

piece of plastic off the beaches in Southern California," Cass had said. "That should take a few centuries."

We hadn't seen any whales yet that day, which had been a bummer, but the dolphins looked to be a nice consolation. As we got closer to them, it became evident that the pod was quite large.

"There must be a hundred!" Summer exclaimed.

"Or more!" Kandace cried. She hadn't been nearly as enthusiastic to go out on the boat as the rest of us, but now, seeing the dolphins, she seemed giddy with delight.

I certainly was. The dolphins weren't bothered by our presence at all. In fact, several of them came right up alongside us and surfed in the wake that our boat created. Their bodies shimmered just beneath the surface of the water. At times they were so close I could have leaned over the edge to pet them. I could see that they had very distinct coloration: their bellies were white, their sides were gray and their backs and fins were black.

"They're spinners!" Cass yelled over the roar of the motors, meaning spinner dolphins. They were the most common dolphins off the coast of California and were named for their habit of leaping from the water. Sure enough, as we watched, one sprang out of the ocean not far ahead of us and twirled in the air.

The largest of the dolphins around us were seven feet

long, although I also spotted some three-footers that were probably less than a year old. No matter their age, they were all surprisingly fast, easily keeping pace with the speedboat as it raced along. Occasionally, another dolphin would burst from the water and spin. It really looked as though they were having fun, enjoying seeing us just as much as we enjoyed seeing them.

"It's a shame Binka couldn't come today," Kandace said. "She would have loved this."

"I think Binka's having a pretty good day anyhow," Summer replied.

Like Trish, Jackson Cross had been happy to turn over evidence against his accomplice to make himself look better; in this case, it was Roswell Crowe. The Colony had quickly turned on Roswell when they learned he'd been destroying beaches all along the coast to shore up Jackson's beach, and so had the neighbors around Roswell's second home in Bel Air. ("It's just more public relations," Cass had noted. "These billionaires burn twenty times the fossil fuel that normal people do to air-condition their ninety-room mansions—and use a hundred times the fresh water to irrigate their giant lawns—but then they turn into huge crusaders for the environment when it makes them look good.")

Roswell had already been under investigation for shady business practices with his construction company.

The revelation that he had also committed environmental crimes had badly weakened his negotiating position for his divorce, and Binka's lawyers had pounced. Binka had gone to her legal firm to renegotiate the contract that day. Her lawyers had gleefully informed her that, by the time they were done, in addition to the Malibu house, Binka might end up with the Bel Air home as well, and maybe even the condo in Aspen.

Meanwhile, many of Jackson Cross's neighbors were threatening to sue him for altering the beach without permission. Chase Buckingham's father, the big-shot lawyer, was leading the charge.

Of course, Chase's father was also suing TransPacific for framing his son—*and* for reckless endangerment and property damage as a result of the exploding whale. Many other residents of the Colony had joined this lawsuit, citing everything from the loss of multimillion-dollar paintings to nervous breakdowns as a result of "volatile cetacean carnage." Cass claimed that the case would certainly take years to settle, but it could ultimately put TransPacific out of business.

"Even better," Cass had said, "it's made the public aware of how much harm the shipping industry can do to marine life. Now that Brock Stoneman is tweeting about how TransPacific killed two whales out of negligence, *millions* of people are taking notice. Maybe that will turn into some actual support for policing shipping lanes—which could even result in more funding for NOAA and other organizations."

I knew there was also a good chance that this *wouldn't* happen, but Cass had a point. Brock Stoneman and the other wealthy residents of the Colony could reach huge sections of the population in ways that other people couldn't. When they talked about things, their followers listened. Ironically, in trying to avoid bad publicity by blowing up the whale, TransPacific had created bad publicity for itself that was a hundred times worse.

After a while, the dolphins got tired of swimming alongside us. Or maybe they simply grew bored of us. The pod veered away from our boat and disappeared into the depths of the ocean.

Cass cut back on the throttle. We slowed down, and the noise of the engines dropped to a low purr so that we no longer had to shout to be heard.

Doc and Kandace took advantage of the lull in the action to sit in the stern of the boat with Cass. Summer and I stayed at the bow, keeping an eye on the ocean, hoping the dolphins might change their minds and come back.

"That was amazing," Summer declared. "Best part of the whole week."

I shot her a sidelong glance. "Even better than getting to meet Wynn Gyoko?"

"Wynn was cool," she replied with a grin, "but he wasn't *that* cool."

"He's the lead singer of one of the biggest bands in the world," I pointed out.

"Yeah, but he hasn't even solved *one* mystery. Whereas my boyfriend has solved so many, I've lost count."

Things had gotten much better between us over the days since the movie premiere. Even though the party itself had ended in disaster, our relationship had come out stronger. After being reminded of what a great team we made, we had apologized to each other for how we had behaved and figured out a compromise to solve our problems. Summer had decided to tweet that she wasn't seeing Wynn Gyoko because she was in a relationship with someone else, but then refused to give any more details, allowing me to keep my life private. The media had instantly gone bananas, wondering who Summer's secret boyfriend was, which ended up getting her even more followers than she'd had when everyone thought she was dating Wynn.

That had forced us to change some of our vacation plans. Kandace had wanted to take us to some fancy restaurants and do some more shopping in Beverly Hills, but now we couldn't for fear of being hounded by the paparazzi. Instead, we needed to lie low, spending most of our days on beaches and hiking trails—which was perfectly fine with both Summer and me.

However, we did have two special things planned for the days ahead. Doc had arranged a behind-the-scenes tour of the San Diego Zoo Safari Park for us—and we were supposed to have lunch with Suzanne Patmore and her creative executives to discuss optioning the story of our crime-solving adventures.

It seemed that the dolphins weren't coming back, so Summer and I abandoned the bow and joined the others at the stern. We had brought a cooler full of sandwiches and drinks, which the adults were digging into.

"If you think it's beautiful over here," Cass was telling Doc, "wait until you see the Gulf of Baja."

"We're going to Mexico?" Summer asked, excitedly. "Isn't that awfully far for this boat?"

The adults turned to us. Cass looked amused while Doc appeared slightly embarrassed.

"*You're* not going to Mexico," Cass informed her, then pointed to herself and Doc. "*We* are."

"For another sea lion rescue?" I asked.

Now Cass grew even more amused, while Doc grew even more embarrassed.

"You can really be a dummy sometimes," Summer told me.

Finally, I understood. "Oh. It's like a romantic thing."

"Yes," Cass confirmed, and Doc turned redder yet.

Summer looked to Doc. "You finally got up the nerve to ask her out?"

"No," Cass said. "I finally got tired of waiting for him to do it."

"I have plenty of vacation time racked up," Doc explained. "So I decided to extend my trip for another week. After we all go to San Diego, Cass and I are going to keep heading south." Despite his embarrassment, Doc looked as happy as I'd ever seen him. That wasn't saying too much, because Doc was usually crabby, but it was still a good thing.

"I think that's wonderful," Kandace proclaimed.

"So do I," Summer agreed.

"And me," I added.

"Me too," Doc said, looking at Cass, who blushed.

Kandace's phone chirped, indicating she had received a text. She looked at it, then gasped with excitement.

"What is it?" Summer asked.

"It's from Suzanne Patmore's office," Kandace reported. She had been handling details with the studio, since Summer and I were still kids. "They want to know if you'd be open to Brock Stoneman joining the meeting tomorrow. If the movie happens, he'd like to play your father, Teddy. Would you be all right with that?"

"Of course!" I exclaimed, then thought to add, "And I'm sure my dad would be thrilled. Brock's his favorite actor."

I had finally told my parents the truth about everything that had happened during my time in California. There was no way I could have kept it a secret; the chaos at the movie premiere had made the national news. I had to do it twice, since Dad was still in Argentina, and while both had chastised me for not being completely honest with them, I still felt much better afterward. Plus, neither of my parents was quite as upset as I had thought they might be. If anything, Mom was upset at *Doc* for dragging me into the investigation. I knew she had called him and given him an earful, but he was in such a good mood because of Cass, he took it all in stride.

"This is turning out to be quite a trip," Kandace observed.

"Sure is," Summer agreed. "Teddy has solved two crimes, destroyed a movie premiere, seen a whale explode, and gotten a movie deal." She looked to me and teased, "Good thing your house burned down."

"You'll be getting a new one soon enough," Kandace said. "J.J.'s on it. He's having brand-new top-of-the-line trailers delivered for your family and everyone else as soon as he can. By the time school starts, you'll have a home again. And until then, you and your family are welcome to stay with us."

"Thanks," I told her. The last week certainly hadn't been

perfect, but it *had* been a good trip, overall. Even though we hadn't seen a—

"Whale!" Summer shouted, pointing off the port bow.

Sure enough, a telltale spout of mist hung in the air a few football fields away from us. A second later, a second spout erupted close by.

"There's another!" Doc exclaimed.

"All right! We've got some blues!" Cass leaped to the wheel and fired up the engines.

Summer and I ran to the bow so we'd have the best view possible.

"You know, Teddy," she said. "Life is always interesting when you're around."

"Is that a compliment?" I asked.

"You bet it is." Summer beamed at me in a way that made me feel like the luckiest person alive.

I grabbed her hand, and we looked toward the horizon as our boat sped across the waves, racing toward the largest creatures that had ever lived.

OUR OCEANS ARE IN DANGER!

When I first started researching this book, I thought it might be difficult to come up with a way that humans could kill a whale. But it wasn't long before I realized that there were a startling number of ways that could happen. The sad fact is that we aren't treating our oceans very well—and thus, all their inhabitants are endangered as well.

However, there are things you can do to help. So let's take a look at a few of the problems.

Plastic

As I indicated in this book, the amount of plastic that we are creating—and then dumping into the oceans—is staggering. The best way to fight this is to simply try to reduce the amount of plastic that you use. I know that might not sound so easy, because plastic is everywhere. But you can take steps: Make sure that your family brings reusable bags to the grocery store instead of getting new plastic bags each time. Carry a reusable water bottle instead of buying water in plastic bottles. If you do buy water—or soda or other drinks—buy them in aluminum cans, rather than plastic bottles. (Aluminum can be more easily recycled, over and over again, which is not the case with plastic.) Tell restaurants that you don't need a straw. (Or, if you're getting takeout food for home, tell them you don't need the plastic utensils.). And if you do use plastic . . . recycle it.

Another thing you can do to help with plastic—and all litter—is to participate in a beach cleanup. These are generally run by local organizations (assuming you live near a beach), so you might have to do a little research to figure out who hosts them in your area. (In Southern California, where I am, they are organized by Heal the Bay.) A beach cleanup is good hands-on work—and it can actually make for a rather enjoyable family day at the beach.

Overfishing

There are fisheries that are well managed—and fisheries that aren't. In some places, fish stocks are being wiped out; in others, poorly managed fish farms are polluting the local waters. The Monterey Bay Aquarium has a very helpful guide to sustainable seafood that shows what is good to eat and what isn't. You can find it here: montereybayaquarium.org (as well as some other helpful tips for reducing plastic use).

Climate Change

As our planet heats up due to human behavior, our oceans are changing in ways that we are only just beginning to understand. Coral reefs are bleaching. Food chains are being disrupted. This is a big problem, in part because there are plenty of people who claim that it doesn't exist. (In fact, I can promise you I'm going to get plenty of angry letters and bad online reviews even for mentioning it. It's happened before.) On one hand, this needs to be tackled on a global level, which means making your voice heard: pressuring your legislators to support alternative fuels like solar and wind energy, or to build more public transportation. You might think that such people don't care about what someone your age thinks, but I think they might be more likely to listen to you—and your friends and classmates—than they are to listen to someone my age.

And there are steps you can take at home: Conserve energy whenever possible. Buy much of your food locally and try to cut down on food waste as well. Donate old clothes and other items rather than throwing them away—and maybe try to buy secondhand clothes yourself. Ask your family to drive hybrid or electric vehicles. Every little bit helps.

Finally, there are still some direct threats to whales and dolphins as well. While most countries in the world have banned the hunting of these amazing creatures, a few countries still have not. To that end, there are many organizations that do important work to protect these species. I'd recommend supporting Sea Shepherd, a group of incredibly devoted

Acknowledgments

It is very common for readers to suggest possible storylines for my books, and I have to give most of them the sad news that I can't really accept ideas from other people. But every once in a while, when I spot a trend in the requests, I have to take notice.

That was the case with this book. A *lot* of young readers asked me to write a FunJungle mystery involving marine life. Many specifically asked about whales, but others simply thought I should write about a crime happening to a sea creature. And since there's an awful lot of marine life, I figured I would consider it.

That involved research. And so I am indebted to Paola Camacho, who did a great amount of that for me, as well as tracking down some specialists for me to talk to. One of those was James Stewart, the whale expert and boat programs coordinator at the Aquarium of the Pacific in Long Beach, California, whose advice and knowledge were invaluable. (Also, thanks to Marilyn Padilla and everyone else at the aquarium for their help). Then there's Dave Bader, chief operations officer at the Marine Mammal Care Center, Los Angeles, who was kind enough to let me (and my daughter) visit his facility and answer all my questions. Without the help of these people, this book would never have existed.

This is also the first book I've ever written that takes place in the city where I live. So I suppose that thanks are long overdue to the people who originally supported me in my film career (which was what kept me busy out here until I started writing middle-grade fiction): Warren Zide, Craig Perry, Sheila Hanahan-Taylor, Craig Titley, David Prybil, Ash Shah, Alan Bursteen, and Tracey Trench. Thanks are also due to my close friends (and support group) from the newer chapter of my writing career, my fellow authors (and other book people): Rose Brock, James Ponti, Julie Buxbaum, Max Brallier, Sarah Mlynowski, Melissa Posten, Gordon Korman, Christina Soontornvat, Karina Yan Glaser, Julia Devillers, Jennifer E. Smith, Adele Griffin, Anna Carey, Leslie Margolis, and Morgan Matson. Particular thanks must be given to Indy Flore for coming up with the title of this book—although several of the other people on this list generated great options (such as "Twist and Spout" and "License to Krill").

On the professional front, there are many wonderful people to thank at my publisher, Simon & Schuster, as well:

Krista Vitola, Justin Chanda, Lucy Ruth Cummins, Erin Toller, Beth Parker, Roberta Stout, Kendra Levin, Alyza Liu, Anne Zafian, Lisa Moraleda, Jenica Nasworthy, Chava Wolin, Chrissy Noh, Ashley Mitchell, Brendon MacDonald, Nadia Almahdi, Christina Pecorale, Victor Iannone, Emily Hutton, Emily Ritter, Theresa Pang, Dainese Santos, and Michelle Leo.

Also, thanks to my intern, Lilian Liu, and to RJ Bernocco and Mingo Reynolds at the Kelly Writers House at the University of Pennsylvania for continuing this great program. And finally, I couldn't get any of this done without my amazing assistant, Emma Chanen.

On the home front, thanks (and much love) to Ronald and Jane Gibbs; Suzanne, Darragh, and Ciara Howard—and finally, Dashiell and Violet, the best kids any parent could ever ask for.